DOUBLE CROSS

PASHA

NEWMAN SPRINGS PUBLISHING
320 Broad Street
Red Bank, NJ 07701

First originally published by Newman Springs Publishing 2021

ISBN 978-1-63692-532-5 (Paperback)
ISBN 978-1-63692-533-2 (Digital)

Printed in the United States of America

This book is dedicated to my grandparents, parents, and the giants who stood up for freedom and equality, whose shoulders I now stand on.

O, MANKIND!

If you have a doubt about the resurrection consider that we created you out of dust, then out of sperm, then out of a leech like clot, then out of a morsel of flesh, partly formed and partly unformed, in order that we may manifest our power to you; and we cause whom we will to rest in the wombs for an appointed term, then we bring you out as babes, that you may reach your age of full strengths and some of you are called to die, and some are sent back to the feeblest old age so that they know nothing after having known much. Further thou seeth the earth barren and lifeless, but when we pour down rain on it, It is stirred to life, and swells, and then it puts forth every kind of beautiful growth in pairs. This is so, because God is the reality and it is he who gives life to the dead and it is he who has power over all things.

(Sura22 Iyat5)

A view of a beautiful, well-kept suburban neighborhood early morning in Mobile, Alabama. Hundred-year-old southern pine trees line the streets, all the houses newly built. This affluent community, having sprung up as a result of the civil right's movement years earlier, pays tribute to the diversity of American culture, and the harmonious intentions of desegregation and equal opportunity. Two children, a little girl named Eunique, and her older brother, Kazi, are at the neighborhood store purchasing candy, and a kite for Kazi. Eunique is standing at the counter next to her brother, looking over the counter at the kites, candies, and other tasty treats.

Eunique is seven years old, a very pretty girl with jet black curly hair pulled into a ponytail. Her facial features and bright, almond-shaped eyes are like her mother's. She has her favorite pair of jeans on, BLACK CHUCK TAYLOR gym shoes and her NBA DARRYL DAWKINS jersey. She also has on Kazi's blue baseball cap turned backward. He gave it to her as a gift, and the first thing she does, when she awakes in the morning is put it on. "I want a kite too, brother!" she says.

Kazi turns to her. "How much money you got?" he asks.

"Six dollars."

"You don't have enough," says Kazi.

"Well, give me some of your money, I'll pay you back, I promise!" says Eunique with a big smile as she gently pulls on her brother arm.

"You'd better, Eunique," says Kazi. He then turns back to the store clerk. "Give me that one for my sister please."

The store owner, a South African immigrant with salt and pepper hair and alert eyes, moved to mobile during the height of apartheid in his country. He steps over to get Kazi's selection then moves over to the cash register as Kazi places the money for the items on the counter. Kazi is the spitting image of his father. He's eleven years old, his hair is cut short, tapered on the sides. He has on his Doctor-J NBA basketball warm up suit, shoes, and jersey to match. He's tall and unusually muscular for his age with sleepy eyes and a warm smile. He allows his sister to step up in front of him at the counter. The store owner places the items in a bag, then hands Kazi his change. "There you go, my little friends, and come again!" he says.

Eunique takes the bag. "Thank you," she replies. They both turn and exit the store. Once outside, Kazi gets on his bicycle, a burgundy twelve-speed Fuji, he then helps his sister on, before handing her the bag. As they make their way home around the corner, their laughing and singing, "You down with OPP yea, you know me!"

They reach their street then head toward their home. Just after doing so, an old blue racing car that's been souped up, turns the corner. It pulls up behind them rolling slowly. Two white skinheads are in the car. Skull, the driver, has on jeans and a black leather vest. Tattoos are all over his arms and chest. Skull is skinny, wiry looking, about twenty-four years old. He's clean-shaven, with a blue tattoo of a human skull, with red eyes on the left side of his neck. He looks over at his buddy reckless, who is watching Kazi and Eunique as they are riding up in front of them.

Reckless has on a matching leather vest, and his body is also covered with tattoos. He has a wild, psychotic look about him—a Charles Manson lookalike with a toothless grin. He takes a quick swig of Jack Daniels from the bottle he was hiding between his legs then wipes his mouth with the back of his hand. "Let's get them, Skull, fuck it. I don't give a damn if they young or old, niggers all the same to me, bro. Hand me the gun from under your seat," he says.

Skull looks over at him, then at Kaze & Eunique. "I don't know, Reckless, man, I don't think it's a good time, let's keep looking."

Inside Kazi and Eunique's home, their father, Malik, has awakened and is coming down the stairs. He's handsome with a strong jawline, medium build, smooth brown complexion, with a body of a natural athlete. He's forty-eight years old, yet still works out two hours a day. An ex-Marine, with a discipline and self-assurance that comes from surviving many battles in life, including Vietnam. Looking at him, you sense a deep intelligence. He heads toward the kitchen, wearing only his linen black-and-gold-striped pajama bottoms, and Gucci black house shoes. He sees his wife, Sakinah, busy preparing breakfast and walks quietly up behind her giving her a kiss on the neck. "Good morning, love of my life, where are the children?" he asks.

Sakinah turns around smiling with the mixing bowl spoon in her hand. "They went around the corner to get some glue or something for Kazi's kite, they should be on their way back." Sakinah turns back to what she was doing, as Malik rubs his hands over her hips and thighs from behind. Sakinah is strikingly beautiful, with big, brown, almond-shaped eyes.

She has a gorgeous smile, with perfect white teeth and luscious full lips. Sakinah is forty-seven years old with a figure most women envy, yet she is humbled by it. She wears no makeup; her complexion is flawlessly golden tan. Her hair, black and silky is styled long on one side, and short on the other, cut in a box style in the front to highlight her facial features. She's tall and leggy, with small delicate hands. "Stop, you know our son doesn't like you kissing all over his mother." She turns around to face Malik then kisses him on his nose. "Well, you know our daughter doesn't like you harassing and depriving her daddy." They laugh and smile together.

"I'm surprised that they didn't wake me up?" says Malik. Sakinah moves away from him over to the stove. Where she spoons pancake batter out of the bowl, into the frying pan. "They tried, Malik, but you were sound asleep," she says.

Malik takes a seat at the kitchen counter. "I worked my buns off on the Rollie Schuster case all day yesterday, we may lose this one. I didn't get in until late."

Sakinah turns around to face him with a mischievous grin on her face. "Yes, you were late getting in." She gives him a sly smile.

Malik looks at her and smiles to himself. "You've got a dirty mind," he says.

They both laughed. "Yes, but that's why I'm fixing you a wonderful breakfast. You've got more work to do this afternoon after the children go over to your moms." Malik smiles then goes over to the refrigerator to get a Evian bottled water out before turning back to his wife. "You're so nasty," He says with a smile as he walks over to Sakinah, stopping to pat her on her bottom.

"You made me that way, big head," says Sakinah.

"No, I brought it out of you."

Outside Skull and Reckless are coming up on the side of Kazi and Eunique. Kazi tries to pedal faster. His sister is scared and clinging to her brother. "They're going to run us over, Kazi!"

"No, they're not!" shouts Kazi. The back window comes down as skull pulls up alongside of them. A gun comes out and both Kazi and Eunique scream! Kazi tries to turn up on the curb, but the first shot rings out striking him in the back of the head; his sister screams. "Kazi!"

They both fall off the bike, Kazi is dead. Eunique is screaming, crying, covered in blood, trying to help her brother up, still holding on to the bag.

"Kazi get up, you're going to be okay," she says, before screaming. "Daddy! Daddy!"

Skull stops the car then backs up a little so that he's beside Eunique; she looks up at him and reckless shoots her in the head. She falls over dead, reckless laughs. "Damn, did you see that? Let's get the fuck out of her!" he yells. Skull then pushes the pedal to the floor and roars up the street, turning the corner.

At that very moment inside their home, Malik and Sakinah stop what they were doing. "Sakinah, was that a gun shot?" Malik asks.

"I don't know, maybe your shorties bought some fire crackers?" says Sakinah. Malik stands, listening with a puzzled look on his face. "No, that sounded like gun shots," he says.

Malik heads for the front door, opens it, then steps outside. Sakinah follows. Malik walks out to the end of his driveway, looks left; he doesn't see anything, then looks right. He then sees Kazi's bike at the curb and what appears to be the bodies of his children. "Oh, God, no! Kazi! Eunique!" he yells before racing to them along with Sakinah, who after seeing they've been shot in the head, and are lifeless, stops a short distance away and falls to her knees crying, staring at her children and their father. Malik is talking to them as he checks them for signs of life. But instantly, he discovers that there is no life, they are gone. Malik looks to the sky. "Please, Allah, don't take my babies from me!" he screams before scooping them up to his chest, holding them in his arms. "Hold on, you two, hold on! Somebody call for help!" he yells.

Some of the neighbors have come outdoors to see what's going on. The men run over to help Malik, but he just sits there covered in blood, rocking his children. The women gather around trying to comfort Sakinah, but it's no use; she doesn't hear them, she's in shock. In the distance, sirens are heard. Sakinah's neighbor and best friend, Lenora Stanton drops her laundry basket then runs over to Sakinah from across the street. She stops and stares in horror as she sees Malik. "Oh my God!" she says, placing her hand over her mouth as the tears begin to flow.

Slowly she walks over to Sakinah and leans down beside her. "Sakinah, Sakinah, honey, come on, let me take you back into the house. You don't need to see this," she says. Lenora places her arm around Sakinah as other ladies from the neighborhood stand by crying talking among themselves, asking who could have done this.

As the 911 call is received and relayed to the police department and then units in the area, Detectives Tracey Brooks and Steve Taylor overhear the dispatcher then signal that they too are responding to the call. Detective Brooks has a puzzled look on his face. "Steve, who would shoot two children in the head from close range!" he asks.

Detective Taylor turns on his siren and goes around a car stopped in front of him. "An animal! An animal that needs to be caught and put to death, Tracey!" They continue the rest of the way to the scene in silence.

CHAPTER 1

Back at the murder scene, almost everyone from the community has gathered around Malik and Sakinah, most are in their bath robes, house coats, and pajamas. None of them can convince Malik to let go of the children. An ambulance has arrived along with eight police cars to secure the area. The paramedics are talking with Malik, trying to get him to release the children so that they can check their vital signs. "Sir, can we take a look at them. Sir! Please, can we check them?"

Malik doesn't even look up. "They're gone." Malik continues holding his children, clearly in a daze. Two police supervisors arrive at the scene. Lieutenant Brian Jackson, a tall heavyset, dark-skinned officer with wavy hair, and a pronounced gap between his two front teeth. A sixteen-year homicide investigator, Jackson knows this drill by heart. Captain Paul Twyman, Jackson's supervisor, has also arrived. Twyman is a twenty-year veteran; he's tall, muscular, with a three-inch slash coming down the middle of his forehead as a reminder not to drink and drive. They both see Malik then shake their heads in disbelief. "Let's go, Lieutenant, that must be the father," says Twyman. They begin moving through the crowd, asking, "Did anyone see what happened?" As they move toward Malik, they come across Sakinah.

Twyman stops then stoops down in front of her. "Ma'am, I'm Captain Paul Twyman, and this is Lieutenant Brian Jackson. Is that your husband and children over there?" he asks.

Sakinah doesn't respond. "Ma'am, we want to try and find out what happened here and the people responsible for it, but we are going to need any help you can give us in doing this." Silence. "Ma'am, is that your husband over there?" the captain asks gently.

Sakinah nods her head yes.

"Ma'am, did you see who did this?"

"No, we heard a shot, but I thought it was a firecracker at first. Malik and I came outside to check and—" Sakinah breaks down, crying again.

The captain stands up and begins talking to Jackson. "This is going to cause a lot of problems," he says. "That word does nothing to describe what's up ahead," says Jackson. Twyman looks at the steady growing crowd and yells to his officers. "Get those people out of here, back into their homes. You can all see her later. We may need her to be examined by a doctor first. Please go home, she will be fine. We won't let anything happen to her."

Lenora hugs Sakinah, gives her a kiss, then stands up. "I'll be over in a little while," she says. Slowly, she turns and walks toward her home, holding back her tears. fighting the impulse to run and scream. Lenora is very pretty. Full lips, slanted brown eyes, shoulder-length black hair, petite, with a great smile, and gorgeous legs. She stops at the top of the stairs to her home and turns to look at all that is taking place. She suddenly has the urge to vomit. Covering her mouth, she runs into her home, slamming the door behind her.

At that moment, Detectives Brooks and Taylor are pulling up at the scene. They pause a moment before getting out of their car. "Steve, can you believe this?" Tracey asks.

Steve reaches for the handle to open his door. "No matter how many times I see it, it never gets easier," he says.

They both get out of the car and head over toward Malik. As they approach, one of the paramedics comes up to Detective Taylor. "We have been trying to get him to release the children for twenty minutes. But he has ignored us and refuses to let them go. When we got here, it was too late, there was nothing we could do," he says. Taylor looks at Malik. "I'll see if we can help, what is his name?" Taylor asks.

"Malik, Malik Davenport."

Taylor and Brooks move over to Malik. Taylor kneels down beside him. Detective Taylor is six-foot-four, lean and mean, dark complexion, with a short afro, which he refuses to cut or style. He and Brooks have known each other since Creveling Elementary School. "They are beautiful, what are their names?" Taylor asks.

Silence.

"How old are they?" Malik does not respond; he simply continues to rock his children. "Mr. Davenport, I'm sure you know that if we are going to solve this, we are going to need your help and cooperation. The longer we sit here, the more time the people who done this have to get away," says Taylor.

Malik looks up. "His name is Kazi." Malik moves the arm holding his son. "He's eleven years old. Her name is Eunique, she's seven. She's my baby girl. They loved each other so much. They done everything together. See, she still has her brother's baseball cap. She loved that cap. She looked up to her brother." Tears are running down Malik's cheeks. "Kazi was so protective of her, he didn't even like for her mom or me to punish her." Silence. "Someone shot my babies in the head."

Malik lets the detectives see…he's in shock, soaked in blood. Taylor can hardly speak. "Uh, Mr. Davenport, we need you to allow the paramedics to do their job so that we can move on with the investigation. The coroner will meet us at the hospital."

Malik doesn't respond, so Taylor motions for the two paramedics to come over. "Give him a hand placing his children in the ambulance," says Taylor. The paramedics look at each other in wonderment since the children are already dead. But they read the expression on Taylor's face and move over to Malik. "Let us give you a hand, Mr. Davenport," says both of the paramedics.

As the children are being loaded in the ambulance, Captain Twyman and Lieutenant Jackson are attempting to get Sakinah up and back into her home. Jackson reaches down for her. "Mrs. Davenport, we'd like to escort you back into your home now. Your husband is going with the ambulance to handle all the issues with the children. Do you have a doctor we can call or a close family member to come stay with you until your husband returns? Come on, let me help you up," says Jackson.

Sakinah doesn't move; she sits watching her husband and children being loaded into the ambulance. After the door closes, the siren blasts, and the vehicle begins slowly weaving through the crowd of people. Suddenly, without saying a word, Sakinah stands then walks to her home, closing the door behind her.

Detective Taylor and Brooks walk over to the Captain and Lieutenant and begin comparing notes. "Captain, Lieutenant, what do we have here, some kind of gang activity?" Detective Taylor asks.

"Steve, I'm not sure, it appears that we have at least two people involved, because the children were shot at the curb on this side of the street. I doubt that the shooter could have driven the car on the wrong side of the street and shot the children at the same time. Look at those tire marks next to the bike." Jackson looks up from his notes. "I spoke to several neighbors who all say that they heard at least two loud pops but thought they were some of the kids outside with firecrackers or some kind of kids toy because there are no shootings or gang activity in this neighborhood. In fact, it was the sound of the tires that caused most of them to look outside."

Brooks is standing there, shaking his head. Detective Brooks is the giant in the department, about six-foot-seven, flat-footed, with a large head and big hands. Nevertheless, he professes to be a ladies' man, and the best detective in the state. "I believe that this was a hate crime. The reason why I say this is because both children were shot almost point-blank one after the other with a forty-five-caliber or nine-millimeter handgun. To use such a weapon on a child, you would have to have a lot of rage inside you."

The officers all look at brooks, engrossed in the sense of what he's saying. "Secondly, there appears to be no apparent attempt to remove the children from the area, as would be the case with a child molester or kidnapper. They were simply shot and left to die," says Brooks.

Taylor turns to the captain. "What does Mr. Davenport do for a living? Maybe the killing was indirectly aimed at him."

"Mr. Davenport is a senior partner at the law firm, Graham, Bell, Harris, and Davenport. He started at the firm as a paralegal intern and worked his way up to partner." Twyman puts his notebook away then continues. "The firm is basically into corporate litigation, mergers, etc. The neighbors I spoke with all said good things about him and his family, and can think of no reason why anyone would harm him on his children."

Lieutenant Jackson agrees. "Not only that, but if this was anything more than a random shooting, it would mean that someone was stalking the Davenports, and as close as these neighbors are here, someone would have noticed that immediately." The captain tosses his hands up in the air. "We are going to head down to the station to see if Mr. Davenport knows anyone who might want to harm him or his family. In the meantime, I'll instruct the remaining officers to continue going door to door, and to check with the owner at the store the children purchased their items from to see whether or not anyone seen them being followed or anything out of the ordinary."

"While that is being handled," says Brooks, "Steve and I are going to see if we can talk to Mrs. Davenport."

"Okay then," says the captain. The officers split up, Twyman and Jackson heading toward their car, but as they proceeded, they notice a neighbor has picked Kazi's bike up out of the street, while another is hosing the blood stain away. The detectives walk over to the Davenports' home and Brooks knocks on the door. There is no answer; he knocks again. Brooks looks back at Taylor who gives the "I don't know" look. Brooks turns back to the door. "Mrs. Davenport, it's Detective Brooks and Taylor, we'd like to speak to you briefly before we begin our search for the people responsible."

Silence. There is no reply.

"Mrs. Davenport, are you okay?"

Silence. Taylor nudges him.

"Maybe we should talk to Mr. Davenport," says Brooks. They turn to leave but the door slowly opens. They step inside as Sakinah walks into the living room and curls up in a chair; she's still crying. The detectives look at all the photos of the family together, camping, swimming, horseback riding. The photo in front of Sakinah is of

Kazi, riding Eunique on his bicycle. Detective Taylor walks over to the chair closes to Sakinah, then he takes a seat. "They're beautiful, I know this is very difficult for you. I have three children of my own, two girls and one son. I would grieve heavily if something ever happened to them…Mrs. Davenport." Taylor slides to the edge of his seat. "Your children are with God now, and there is nothing you or I can do about that." He claps his hands together. "I wish I could. But the people who done this, they are still here, they're out there somewhere, and we are going to find them."

Sakinah looks up briefly at the detective before dropping her gaze back to the photo of her children.

"But before we begin our search. I need to ask you some questions so that we can try to find a starting point for our search. Do you understand this, Mrs. Davenport? Your children need you to be strong so that we can bring the people that done this to them to justice. Can you muster enough strength for that?"

"Yes," says Sakinah without looking up.

"Okay, let's start by you telling us how long you and your husband have been married?" Detective Brooks takes out his notepad then his pen as he prepares to take notes.

"Malik and I were childhood sweethearts. We met while we were in the seventh grade. After graduating from high school, we both attended Howard University in DC. I majored in marketing and Malik majored in corporate law. We got married after graduating. Malik went off to Vietnam with the Marines. When he returned, we moved here to Mobile because Malik's auntie Patricia Harris is senior partner at the law firm that he now works for. It's been in his family for four generations, it was started by his great grandmother, Ruth Bell and her father Judge Graham."

Brooks looks up from his notes. "Mrs. Davenport, how long have you lived here?"

"Thirteen years," says Sakinah.

"Have you or your husband ever had any problems with your neighbors, either racial or otherwise?" Brooks asks.

"No! All my neighbors and my family have been close since we moved here. We celebrate together. We attend each other's children birthday parties, backyard barbecues, and we watch out for each other's home and property when someone is away. My neighbors know when Malik and I are away, and if I can't pick the children up, they stay with Lenora, and her son Kevin until Malik or I arrive home."

Taylor gathers his thoughts. "Mrs. Davenport, has your husband ever told you that he has been threatened by anyone? He or his firm?"

"No, Malik is very well liked among his peers and the community. He volunteers his time to help feed the homeless. He's a mentor and a Big Brother to children without fathers. Every summer he takes a bus load of children from the Orange Grove Project's and the John Park area, camping at his expense."

Brooks holds his pen up. "One last question, Mrs. Davenport. Where were you and your husband when you heard what you initially thought were fine crackers?"

"In the kitchen," says Sakinah.

"Where does Ms. Stanton live?" Brooks asks.

"Directly across the street."

"Is there anyone else who spends a lot of time with the kids. Someone they might have told secrets too, that maybe they would not tell you or their father?" asks Taylor. "Maybe there was a bully at the store or someone new in the neighborhood Kazi was afraid of and never said anything about? We want to check every possible lead. Kids as young as age seven have been known to take guns to school and shoot innocent people," he says.

They both spoke candidly with Ms. Norma, their grandmother, she lives at sixty-eight Raymond Avenue. That's Malik's mom. Both my parents are deceased. My only close relative here is my brother," says Sakinah.

"Thank you, we will try to solve this as quickly as possible." Brooks and Taylor stand to leave, while Sakinah remains seated. They find their way back to the door, closing it behind them. Once outside, the detectives head toward their car; Brooks looks over at Taylor. "If what she says is true, we have no clear motive for this," he says.

"Yeah, but whoever done this to those children had a motive, you don't shoot children," says Brooks.

"Let's start with the grandmother," says Taylor. "Then head back to the station to speak with Mr. Davenport and the captain."

As the detectives are pulling off, Lenora is calling for her son Kevin to come downstairs. He's been in his room since the shootings. Worried that she gets no response, she goes up to his room, opens the door, and peeps in. "Kevin, are you all right?" She calls him again, "Kevin!" Lenora walks over to his closet door and opens it. Kevin is sitting in there, trembling and crying. Kevin is small for his age and looks just like his mom, but with big dark eyes.

"Baby, what are you doing in there?" she asks. Lenora steps inside the closet, taking a seat beside Kevin then wrapping her arms around him. "I know you loved Kazi and Eunique and you're going to miss them, but, honey, they are both in heaven now. They're not hurting anymore." She wipes his tears away. "I'm sure they would want you to be okay." Kevin does not respond. "Why don't you come on downstairs and let me fix you something to eat." Lenora looks closely at her son. "Kevin, you're trembling, what's wrong?" she asks. Frustrated, she places her hand on his forehead. "You have a fever, I'm calling the doctor!" Lenora scoops him up then rushes out of the closet and into her bedroom where she reaches for the phone.

It's early afternoon, Malik is sitting in the office of Captain Twyman in silence. The captain is talking on the phone. He finishes his call, stands, then walks outside of his office to speak to Detective Taylor and Brooks, who have just arrived. Brooks stops in front of him. "We spoke with Mrs. Davenport and some of her neighbors. We have no motive for the shooting," he says.

"I just got off the phone with ballistics," says Twyman. "Both of the children were shot with a forty-five-caliber pistol. Ballistics believes that the boy was shot first, as he was pedaling home because he was shot on the right side of his head. With the direction his bike was facing at the scene, that would place his home on the left. They believe the little girl was shot as she attempted to help her brother that she looked up at the shooter, thus the reason for being shot in the front of the head."

Taylor clenches his fist. "Damn! I cannot wait until I get my hands on this piece of trash!" The captain changes the subject. "Why don't you guys see if you can find a change of clothes for Mr. Davenport, he still has those bloody clothes on. I'll see if he can add anything else and we'll get him home to his wife, then meet later."

The captain walks back into his office, closing the door behind him, retaking his seat. Captain Twyman has run the Mobile Police Department for ten years, and he's seen his share of bloody scenes. He can recall his own experiences as a child growing up in Alabama in the forties, when no blacks were safe—man, woman or child. He looks at Malik.

"Mr. Davenport, I just have a couple more questions for you, and I will get you home. Mr. Davenport, can you think of anyone who may have wanted to hurt your family?"

"No!" says Malik. As he looks down at his hands covered in his children's blood.

"Has there been any unusual events in your life, or the community you live in?"

"No."

"Have any strangers been seen or any burglaries been reported in the past few months?"

"No!"

"Mr. Davenport, I'm going to have a car take you home now, your wife is there alone, and I believe you need each other now. We are very sorry for your loss."

The captain stands and walks around his desk to the door. "Jackson is there with the change of clothes." He offers them to Malik. "Mr. Davenport, I think these will fit you," he says.

"No, thank you," says Malik as he walks by the detectives and on out the door. People in the station stare in horror.

CHAPTER 2

The doctor is at the Stanton home, in Lenora's bedroom with Kevin. He turns to her as she reenters the room. "Ms. Stanton, Kevin is running a fever. However, he has no other symptoms of a cold or flu. His fever appears to be the result of his fear. Did he see the children who were killed?" he asks.

"Maybe, from a distance, I believe he was in the living room watching cartoons when I ran out." She turns to her son. "Kevin, did you see what happened today?" she asks.

Kevin pulls the blanket up over his head. The doctor turns to Lenora. "I believe Kevin definitely seen something," he says. Lenora stands there looking at her son, her eyes watering.

FBI agents, Clayton Oliver and John Branch are sitting at their favorite sports bar watching the news coverage of the murders over drinks and a late lunch. They hear the TV anchor say that there are no suspects or motives for the murders. They look at each other. Clayton is the taller of the two, dark-skinned and broad-shouldered. He is also the more aggressive of the two. John is medium height, light skin, wide nose, big ears, the analyzer of details. They both have nine years' experience as agents, as well as prior military experience. Oliver, the army, Branch, the marines. They make an interesting team of pro and cons.

Oliver turns to Branch. "John, are you thinking what I'm thinking."

"Yep!" says Branch.

"Let's go see Chief Jacocks," says Oliver.

"I can think of an entire nation of suspects," says Branch. They both get up to leave, dropping the cost of their meal on the counter as they head out to their car. Oliver is driving. Once inside they begin discussing their suspicions. Branch turns to Oliver. "Clayton, you know very few people in this country are aware of the cover up the Justice Department, the US Attorney General, the Local Law Enforcement in Atlanta, and the White House, used in the Atlanta child murders?" says Branch.

"I know," Oliver agrees. "They still believe Wayne Williams was the killer."

"Yeah, and all the conspirators have worked hard all these years to keep it that way and to keep that man in prison as the fall guy to prevent what they thought could very easily have become a race riot in America," says Branch.

"And yet they knew all the while that the Klan was behind it. This shit is so fucked up, man. A thousand times I've thought about turning in my badge," says Oliver in disgust.

"Me too," says Branch. "But if we don't keep an eye on things, they may get way out of hand."

"So true," says Oliver as he merges into the highway traffic.

Malik has just arrived at his home. He exits the police car, goes up to his door, which is unlocked and walks inside. Sakinah is still sitting on the couch, being comforted by her brother Hugh Lamont, who sees Malik enter. "Malik!" he calls.

Malik looks over at them but walks up the stairs without answering. He goes into the bathroom, closing the door. Moments later, the sound of the shower being turned on is heard in the quiet of the house. An hour later, the bathroom door opens. Malik comes down the stairs in black sweat pants and a black top. He walks into the living room and stands in front of Sakinah. She stands up and they embrace. Both of them crying uncontrollably. Hugh Lamont doesn't know what to do. He stands up, grabbing his jacket.

"I'll leave you two alone now, but if you need me to do anything. If you need me to help with arrangements, just give me a call. Sis, stay strong."

Hugh is six-feet-four around two hundred and sixty pounds, with shifty eyes. As a child, he was always picked on and compared to the cartoon character "Baby Hughey" because of his big wide behind, and his first name, which was also his father's first name. He touches them both on their shoulders before leaving.

Sakinah pulls back to look Malik in his face. "What are we going to do? Who would do such a thing to children? They never hurt anyone!" she says.

"I know, baby, I know we will find out who done this, and I promise you that I am going to kill them. Kill them for sure," says Malik. He takes her face in his hands. "We have a lot to do to send our babies off right, so we must pull ourselves together for them, and get busy solving this mystery, can you do this, Sakinah?" he asks.

"I don't know, I don't have any strength," she says, placing her head back on Malik's shoulders and hugging him tightly. "We will let my mom and your brother handle the arrangements for the funeral. I'll take the phone off the hook, and you and I can just sit here for a while, okay?"

"Okay, whatever you decide, baby."

Sakinah begins to cry again, Malik sits her down on the sofa, then walks over to the phone and takes it off the hook, he turns the lights off and comes back to the sofa and sits down with his wife.

They both sit there holding each other, absorbed in the thought of the death of their children.

FBI Agents Branch and Oliver pull up at the suburban home of their FBI station chief, Clarance Jacocks. It's nearly 4:00 p.m. Agent Branch looks over at his partner. "You think the boss has been monitoring this?" he asks.

"I'd bet my life on it," says Oliver. "Let's go."

They get out of the car, walk up to the door and ring the bell. The chief's wife Tammy opens the door.

"Hello, Clayton, John, come in!" she says.

They both greet her with hello. Agent Oliver walks in first. "Is the chief in, Tammy?" he asks.

"Yes, he is, make yourselves comfortable, I'll get him for you." As Tammy heads upstairs, the agents begin looking at the array of photos of their chief and his wife. Though Tammy won't tell her age, she looks to be around thirty-five years old. A model's body, long natural eyelashes with curly, jet-black hair, cut very short. From the photos you can tell that she is a woman that loves life. Oliver looks over at Branch.

"The chief is a very lucky man," he says. Branch nods in agreement. Moments later, Clarance comes downstairs. The chief is fifty-four years old, his hair shows signs of graying on the sides, but he is in amazingly good shape for his age. He's slimly built, which he attributes to his days as a wrestler himself and later as a coach at John Sherman Junior High for several years. He's dark, with piercing light brown eyes.

"Well, if it isn't my two favorite crime stoppers. Don't tell me you two couldn't find anything to do on this bright sunny day?" he asks.

Agent Oliver smiles. "Chief, John and I were wondering if you had seen the news story on the Davenport children today?"

"Yes, I've seen that. Tammy has been crying off and on all day because of it." Agent Branch turns to the chief.

"You know they have no motive and no suspects. Clayton and I were thinking—"

The chief interrupts him, "I know what you were thinking, but until we get more information, this is not an FBI case. It's a local case, plain and simple. It's their investigation," he says.

"We know, but sill Clayton and I were wondering if we could monitor the investigation from a distance and maybe talk to the detectives on the case?"

"That is entirely up to you and the detectives working the case. Just as long as it doesn't interfere with Bureau policies." The chief gives them both the old evil eye.

"Thank you, sir, we will keep you posted," says Branch. They both get up to leave and Clarance walks them to the door. Closing it behind them he stands there momentarily smiling to himself then walks back upstairs.

The sun has set, Ms. Norma (Malik's mom) is sitting at her home talking with her best friend Martha Mosley. Ms. Norma has a regal dignity about herself. She's sixty-five years old, yet with the vitality of someone in her forties. She's light-skinned, with a head full of thick gray hair, she's five-foot-seven, bowlegged, bright eyes, and has an aura of authority about her. She is the matriarch of the family, having five younger brothers and sisters, one of which, Alvin, died at a young age from a birth defect.

Martha and her have been friends for over thirty years, beginning back when they both attended Mt. Sinai Baptist Church together, where their husbands, both deacons, were best friends, along with Pastor Witson.

"Martha, some evil person killed both of my grand babies," she says. Ms. Norma is crying, but trying hard to maintain her composure. "Just shot them down like they were animals on the curb!" she screams.

"You just have to keep the faith in the Lord, Norma," says Martha, as she goes over to sit beside Ms. Norma and console her. Martha is black and proud of it. Medium height, curvy hips, and a rich southern accent. She can still turn a few heads, young and old. "He will see us through," she says as she holds Ms. Norma's hand. "We've seen so much evil and death, I just know he's going to make it right soon," Martha suggests.

"I sure hope you're right, I really do," says Ms. Norma. They both sit quietly until Martha breaks the silence. "How are Malik and Sakinah taking this?" she asks.

"Hard, girl, very hard!" says Ms. Norma.

"I can imagine," says Martha.

"There is going to be more killing behind this, that's for sure," says Ms. Norma.

"Why you say that?" Martha asks.

"I just know it." A new wave of tears burst loose from Ms. Norma as she clearly sees the future. Martha wraps her arms around her dear friend as she ponders Ms. Norma's prediction of more killings.

It's the next day; early morning, the sun is rising, and Detective Taylor and Brooks are on the way to the Stanton residence. Taylor is adjusting his tie. "What exactly did Ms. Stanton say?" he asks.

"She didn't say anything," says Brooks.

"I spoke with a Geneva Woodson, her sister-in-law. She says that the boy seen something, possibly the shooters."

"I sure hope so," says Taylor. As the detectives are pulling up in front of the Stanton home, Malik is in the front room of his home finishing up a call with Hugh Lamont. "Listen, Hugh, I don't care what he said, or what it costs, my children are Muslims. I have to prepare them for burial and their coffin must face east! That's it, that's all!" Malik slams the phone down then walks out the door as the detectives get out their car then walk over to Malik standing in his driveway.

Taylor arrives across the street first, "Good morning, Mr. Davenport, how are you feeling?" he asks.

"Numb, but I know I have to keep moving for my wife's sake." Brooks comes up beside Taylor.

"How is your wife doing?" he asks.

"She cried and screamed all night. She's sleeping now and I have a meeting I have to go to, if you would excuse me," says Malik.

Taylor steps to the side. "Sure, we are on our way over to talk with Ms. Stanton. As soon as we have any more information regarding the case we will contact you," he says.

"I'd appreciate it." Malik walks over and open the door of his mint green, four-door Jaguar SJ6, gets in, starts the car, then backs out of the driveway. The detectives watch him for a moment then walk on over to the Stanton home and ring the doorbell. The door is opened by a tall, caramel-skinned woman with a dazzling smile.

"May I help you?" she asks.

"I'm Detective Brooks and this is Detective Taylor, we are here to see Ms. Stanton."

"Oh, okay, come on in and have a seat. I'm Geneva, her sister-in-law, but everyone calls me Gen. Come on in I'm the one who called you."

Taylor and Brooks step inside the home.

"Is her son okay?" Detective Brooks asks.

"Kevin has been running a fever, and he's very afraid, he won't say a word." Gen is visibly upset, but even so Brooks can't help but notice how voluptuous her body is and how those Bill Blast black jeans she's wearing with a short, cut-off red tank top screams, sex-ee. Detective Brooks asks the next question as gently as possible.

"Is he in shock, maybe you should call a doctor?" he suggests.

"Lenora called the doctor to look at him already, he said Kevin's temperature can't be explained, he has no symptoms of a cold or allergies. Both the doctor and his mother believe he seen the shooting," says Gen.

The detectives glance at each other, knowing the other's thoughts. "Let me get her and she can tell you more about it." Gen walks out of the living room then down the hall, leaving the Detectives on pins and needles over the prospect of talking to Kevin. A couple minutes later, Lenora walks into the room, her eyes are swollen from crying and a lack of sleep.

"Hello, I'm Lenora Stanton," she says. Both Detectives stand and introduce themselves. They then sit down with Lenora as she opens the conversation, by informing them of her finding Kevin in the closet.

"Kevin and the Davenport children were very close, they were like his sister and brother," she says. "I knew that what happened would hurt him deeply. I expected that, but there is something else bothering him that he won't talk about. When I asked him did he see what happened, he began to tremble then pulled the cover up over his head." Lenora quickly places her hand over her mouth to quiet a sob.

Detective Taylor moves closer to comfort her. "Where were you at the time of the shooting, Ms. Stanton?" he asks.

"I was doing the laundry, and please, call me Lenora." She tries to muster up a small smile.

"Okay, Lenora, where was Kevin?" Taylor asks.

"As far as I know, he was in here watching television."

Detective Brooks looks up from his notes. "Lenora, when did you know that there had been a shooting?" he asks.

"When I heard all the screaming outside. I had brought a load of clothes up from the basement, and as I turned to go upstairs, I heard the screams and I ran outside."

"Did you see Kevin in here?"

"No, I don't remember. I saw Malik screaming with all that blood. I just don't remember." Lenora begins crying lightly. "I can't seem to recall much of anything these last twenty-four hours," she says.

"That's very understandable," says Taylor.

"May I speak to Kevin?" Taylor asks.

"Sure, he's in my bedroom, come on I'll show you where he is." Lenora stands then heads toward her room as Detective Taylor follows her.

Detective Brooks glances over at Gen nervously as she leans up against the doorway. "I hope Kevin comes through for us," he says.

"He will, he's a good kid. Plus, he loves Eunique and Kazi. He just needs a little time," says Gen.

"Sure he does," says Brooks as he slides back in his chair, making himself comfortable.

CHAPTER 3

Malik is driving up in front of an old, small, one-floor house some-one has fixed up. The house is surrounded by tall trees and bushes. If you did not know where the house was, you'd miss it. Malik blows the horn twice, then sits and waits. Silence.

From the passenger side of the car, two figures emerge from the woods wearing camouflage clothing, black boots, a .45-caliber handgun holstered on the left side of their upper body, with a twelve-inch hunting knife tied down on their thigh. The two peek inside the vehicle without being seen themselves then move around to the driver's door, silently snatching it open!

"Malik!" they scream then burst out with laughter and big smiles. Malik, startled, recovers then gets out the car.

"My brothers, semper fi," he says before giving Amin and Pup a big hug each. Amin and Pup are old service buddies of Malik. All three were in Nam together and have been lifelong friends ever since. Amin, is about six feet six inches, two hundred and eighty pounds, dark-skinned, bald-headed, and strong as a bull! He's second in authority among this group of ex-Marines, next to Malik. A no-non-sense type of guy, out of all the group, he's closest to Malik. It was Malik that went back for him during a firefight when he had been cut off by the Vietcong and left for dead. He's also the Godfather of Kazi and Eunique.

Pup is not only a good friend but also a homie of Malik. Having lived in East Baltimore, they met prior to the war through a lady friend of Malik's, named Murray whom Pup was dating. Ironically, they ended up side by side in Nam. Pup is about the same size as Malik, the quiet, deadly type. He too is dark, clean-shaven, and very observant. After returning from the war, he found societies definition of friendship shallow, so his only friends in the world are his buddies from the war, who are known as "Faze Two." They earned this name because during the war, if the initial battle plan did not work, which usually meant the white boys had the first shot. The commander would then call on Malik and have his squad give it a try.

Pup steps back to look at Malik. "What brings you out here my brother?" he asks.

"Pup, someone murdered both my babies the other day. Shot them point blank in the head and left them to die, right down the block from my home." Malik struggles to control himself. "Whoever done this is about to get it!" says Malik.

Pup walks up to him and they embrace. Amin steps back in disgust. "Uh, no, bro! Not my godbabies?" he says, visibly shaken.

"Yeah, bro." Malik is hurting. He reaches into his car and pulls out a paper bag, then empties the contents out. It's his bloody clothing. "It's blood for blood, bro, blood for blood!" Tears roll down Malik's face as Amin steps up and they too embrace tightly.

"Whatever you say, big bruh," says Pup as he closes the car door.

"So be it, let's go inside and talk," he suggests. All three turn and head toward the house. Malik stops to pick up the blood-stained clothes, placing them back inside the paper bag before following Amin and Pup.

Once inside, they all take a seat. Amin looks over at his friend knowing full well what's about to come. "How is Sakinah doing? I know this has destroyed her," he says.

"Yeah, I believe she's still in shock. I done what I could, said all I could say, but I ran out of words." Malik wipes a forming tear away. "You know after we all left the Core, I never thought I'd see the day when I would long to kill again… I've seen enough blood, death, and misery," says Malik.

Pup nods his head in agreement. "That's why Amin and I are out here, bro. Nothing but peace and quiet and our thoughts. Until now." Pup looks over at Amin who is still struggling with the loss of his godchildren.

"Malik, what do you have in mind," Amin asks.

"Do you know who done this?"

"No, not yet. The police haven't come up with anything yet either. But I've contacted some old friends and asked them to keep their ears to the ground, Mobile is too small. Something will surface."

"What do you want Amin and me to do?" Pup asks.

"Be patient, whoever done this dies my way. They don't get to sit on death row for fifteen to twenty years. They die here, now, no mercy!" Amin and Pup nod their head in agreement. "When that time comes, I want you two with me making it happen," says Malik.

Amin stands up with a mock salute. "Semper fi, till I die, ruff, tuff, can't get enough, amphibious monster, sir!"

Pup stands and adjusts his gun holster. "Mother fuck it! It's like you said, blood for blood."

Back at the Stanton's home, Detective Taylor is sitting in Lenora's bedroom on the bed next to Kevin. His mother is standing at the foot of the bed. "Hello, Kevin, I'm Detective Steve Taylor. You can call me Steve. Your mom tells me that you're not feeling well, that's understandable. It must be hard on you. But guess who else it's hard on? You know who that is? It's hard on Mr. and Mrs. Davenport." Silence. "Yes, they are very hurt because Kazi and Eunique are not here anymore. But their also hurt because the people who done this cannot be punished. Kevin, do you know why they can't be punished?" Kevin continues to look down at the floor. "It's because no one knows who done it, and if they do know, their too afraid to tell. But there is nothing to be afraid of Kevin. Your mom tells me that Kazi and Eunique were like your own brother and sister. Is that true? You were good friends?" Kevin moves his lips a little and nods his head.

"Kazi was older than you, so he protected you like a big brother, huh?" Taylor rubs Kevin on his shoulder. Again, Kevin nods his head. "So if something happened to you, he wouldn't be afraid to tell on the person he seen hurt you would he?" Silence. "And what about Eunique. She was like your little sister, you wouldn't let someone hurt your little sister and get away with it, would you?" Kevin responds so quietly, you can barely hear him.

"No," he says.

"Well, Kevin, that's what's going to happen if you've seen who did that to your big brother and little sister and don't say anything." Kevin pulls the cover up over his head again. Taylor looks back at his mother who is crying.

It's early evening. Malik is driving up in front of a brown stone building with beautiful landscaping. The canopy in white and gold trim reads, "Bonners Funeral Home." Malik gets out the car then walks inside the door. He's greeted by the owner, a smartly dressed blackman who looks very much like Sammi Davis Jr.

"Mr. Davenport, how do you do?" The two of them shake hands. "I'm William Bonner, but please call me Billy and this is my wife, Christine."

Malik steps over to greet her noting that she's also smartly dressed and expertly tailored in her white and gold trim two-piece skirt outfit. Everyone knows this couple, their home is never locked, and they have helped raise many of the children that grew up with their own son and two daughters. Billy is the professor in the community, taking time to talk with the young men trying to find their way. Christine is the mother, stylish, fun loving, giving love to all those in need. And yet she still finds time to play the lottery every day and go to Bingo twice a week.

"How do you do ma'am?" Malik asks.

"I'm okay, I want you and your wife to know that we are deeply grieved over your loss," she says.

"Thank you," says Malik. There's an awkward silence. Billy touches Malik on the shoulder. "If you'd come this way, Mr. Davenport."

Malik follows him as they walk past the chapel, down a hall, then stop at the top of some stairs leading to the basement. As they descend the stairs, Billy begins to ease Malik's mind regarding his request. "Your request is somewhat unusual. We generally clean and dress the bodies of the deceased," he says. "I'm grateful for your understanding. As I told you over the phone, my children are Muslims. Their bodies can only be cleaned and prepared for burial by family, to protect the shame of their nakedness being exposed to strangers, even in death."

"I understand, Mr. Davenport. We've done a good job, however, patching up their wounds," says Billy.

"You have my gratitude, Mr. Bonner," says Malik.

They walk into a darkened room where Billy reaches and turns on the light revealing Kazi and Eunique on separate tables with a sheet pulled up to their necks. Malik walks over between them. "Would you leave us now, Mr. Bonner, I'll call you when I'm done," he says.

"As you wish, Mr. Davenport. Take all the time you need."

Billy leaves as Malik pauses between the two tables, before sitting the black bag he has been carrying on the table at Kazi's feet. "As Salamu Alaikum, my beautiful babies. I know that you hear me and see me. I know you both have a lot to tell me, but Allah has taken your voices in this world. But that's okay, because we will all talk again in paradise. Yes, Kazi, your mom is okay. She misses you both very much, but she knows we will all be family again soon, in a life where there is no evil or death." Malik fights to hold back his tears and to find his voice, but the tears come anyway. "We both know, Kazi, that you tried to protect your sister. We are sure of that! I smile to myself when I picture it, you are quite a young lion and I'm very proud of you. Eunique, my baby. You are so beautiful, your mom and I know that if someone was trying to hurt your brother, that you weren't running anywhere. You are so brave. You two stayed there for each other as you should have and your mom says she's also proud of you both." Malik pauses. "Guess what I brought you?" Malik reaches inside the bag and pulls out Kazi's blue baseball cap, Eunique's favorite. "I knew you would want it with you." Malik sits it at the end of the table then takes both of their hands in his. He stands there allowing the tears to fall freely in silence. Minutes pass by. "I've come to wash you both and to dress you. I know you both think that you are too old for your dad to bath you." He smiles. "But you know what I told you about Janaazah. When a Muslims soul goes back to the one who created it, remember? I have to get you all cleaned up, so you'll be nice and pretty and handsome, when you meet the creator."

Malik begins to take the Kafa (burial clothes) out the bag, and two jugs for pouring water over the bodies. He goes over to the sink and fills two large buckets with warm water. He goes back inside the bag and brings out a container with camphor and one with musk in it. He then empties the contents into the buckets. Malik removes a box of cotton balls, six clean towels, two sponge mittens, and two Satr (private part covers) from the bag. He then begins to wash Kazi, his firstborn first, by taking some cotton balls out, wetting them, then washing the inside of Kazi's mouth out three times, then the inside of both nostrils three times. He dips one of the mittens into the musk and camphor buckets, then washes his face, his arms from wrist to elbow, three times. Right, then left. Then his feet, up to the ankles, three times. Right then left. He then takes more cotton balls and closes up his son's nostrils, ears, and mouth, to prevent water from entering the body.

Malik uncovers Kazi completely and places the Satr over his groin area. He then tilts him on his left side to allow the right side to be washed first. He pours the warm water from head to toe once then washes the entire right side of his son's body, down to the left side. He then pours the water over the body twice more before turning Kazi on his right side and repeating the process. He then lift's Kazi to a slight sitting position and gently massages his stomach with a downward stroke to clear anything in it. He turns Kazi on his left side again and pours more warm water over him, three times. Once completed, he removes the cotton balls from his mouth, ears, nose, and begins to dry him and the table.

This completed, he dresses him in the three pieces of white cloth designated for deceased Muslim males. Malik then repeats the same process with his daughter, concluding with wrapping her in the five piece white cloth designated for the burial of Muslim females. Finished, he stands and looks at them both. "You two look like angels. I miss hearing you two running through the house. I thank you both for giving me and your mom so much love and so many beautiful memories. Who knows, your daddy may see you sooner than you think." Malik kisses them both then turns to leave, turning off the lights.

Back at the Stanton residence, Detective Taylor is still in the room with Kevin talking softly to him. "Kevin, did you see who shot Kazi and Enrique?"

Kevin places his head under the cover. "Yes," he says at a whisper.

Taylor looks down at Lenora who then moves up to sit beside her son. She takes him out from under the covers and places him on her knee. "Baby, what did you see?" she asks.

"I was watching the Superfriends on TV, and I forgot that I had left my Spiderman outside. I...I...opened the door and went to get it, and I saw Kazi coming up the street on his bike with Eunique on the back holding a bag. Then I saw this blue racing car coming up behind them," says Kevin.

Taylor and Lenora lock eyes.

"They were driving on the wrong side." He begins to cry.

Taylor pats him on his knee. "It's okay, Kevin, you're doing real good. What else did you see?" Taylor asks.

Kevin pauses, wipes his eyes, then looks up at his mom, who gives him an assuring smile. "The one guy that was on this side crawled in the back. They rode up to Kazi and Eunique and I heard a loud noise, then I heard a loud pop, and then the car drove off real fast. And I was afraid so I ran upstairs and got in my closet." Kevin buries his face in his mother's chest as she holds him real tight.

"Baby, there ain't nothing to be afraid of, no one is going to hurt you, ever!" she says.

Taylor touches Kevin to get his attention. "Kevin, you say it was a racing car, how do you know that?" he asks.

"Because it had a big motor sticking out the front and a white stripe on the side, with a white skull on the back part."

"Kevin, did you see who was driving the car, can you tell me what he looked like?" Taylor asks.

"It was two white guys with bald heads," says Kevin.

"Are you sure?" asks Taylor.

"Yes."

Lenora kisses Kevin again, as Detective Taylor rubs his head, then gets up to leave the room, returning to the living room where Brooks is talking to Gen. Brooks reads Taylor's expression and stands up.

"Did you find out anything?" he asks.

"Yes, let's go!" says Taylor. Then turning to Gen. "It was a pleasure meeting you, tell Ms. Stanton I'll get back in touch with her and Kevin," he says, as Gen stands then walks the detectives to the door.

"Okay, you two be careful," she says. Brooks turns to her. "We will, and good luck on your job interview." He then walks out the door catching up with Taylor.

"What's up?" he asks. "The boy said he seen a blue racing car with a big motor sticking out the front, with white stripes on the side and a skull on the back," says Taylor.

"Did he get a look at the driver?" asks Brooks.

"Yeah, he said they were two white guys with bald heads, and that one of them climbed in the back as the car came up beside the children, and he heard two loud noises and seen the Davenport children laying by the curb. So he ran in the house."

"So this was racially motivated!" Brooks stops in his tracks.

"Sure, looks that way," says Taylor.

"When do we tell the Davenports?" Brooks asks.

"The funeral is tomorrow, let's wait until after that," says Taylor.

"Well, you'd better let Ms. Stanton know," Brooks suggests.

"You're right, I'll be right back."

As Taylor is rushing back to the Stanton home, Malik drives up into his driveway. He gets out, nods at Detective Brooks, then walks into the house. His cousin and wife's best friend Jada, runs into his arms. The house is full of his family members.

"Malik! Are you all right?" Jada asks.

"Yeah, cuz, I'm holding on."

Jada kisses him, pulls back slightly looking at his face, then kisses him again.

Jada is beautiful, a chip off the old block in a long line of beautiful women from her great-great-grandmother, who was half Apache Indian. Jada has a unique jawbone structure, her doe eyes and pearly white teeth are traits also shared among both sides of the family, paternal and maternal. Malik's father, and all his father's sisters and brothers moved to California when Malik was a small child. He's seen them when he attended Crenshaw High School out in Los Angeles for two years. His grandmother, along with his aunts would always send him, and Kerry, his older brother, gift's, especially at Christmas. Malik can still recall riding around Los Angeles, Compton and Watts with his uncles Ronnie and Erskin. He still has a great love for them all in spite of the distance, and not seeing each other for years. Jada is Malik's mother's youngest sister's daughter. Her father, Mooney, also went to war for America but with the Army. While he was there, his government turned him out on heroin as they did thousands of others. When he finally made it back to the U.S., the same government kicked him to the curb and he was left to fend for himself along with other war veterans…caught between the love for his wife and daughter and the monkey on his back, which kept him broke; he moved from job to job until finally with no hope to be found Mooney ended up where most soldiers used and discarded by the government end up. Prison. So Malik become her father, big brother, friend, and protector.

They both walk into the living room holding each other. Jada's eyes are swollen as are seemingly everyone there. Crying not just over the death of the children, but for Malik and Sakinah who put so much into bringing the family closer together. His other cousin Jasmine comes over and hugs him also. She's Malik's grandmother's oldest sister's granddaughter. Jazz is petite, a bundle full of energy and fun, with a very attractive southern accent. "Malik, I'm here for you, cuz!" She cries lightly on his shoulder.

"I know, Jazz, I know," he says.

While he's standing there with Jada and Jasmine, Jada's mom Patricia comes over. She is the senior partner at their law firm. She kisses Malik. "Son, I know what's going on in your head, but remember what I've always told you. Try to do it the right way first." She hugs him tight and kisses him again. Aunt Pat is a younger version of Malik's mother. She's classy, about five-foot-six, a sturdy figure, full lips, with oval shaped eyes. She treats Malik like the son she never had.

"I remember Auntie Pat, and I will," says Malik.

They all go and sit down among the other family members. Uncle Mack is there, the disciplinarian of the family, he's Malik's grandmother's oldest brother and he will whip anyone's children in the family. He doesn't care who their parents are. A stickler for cleanliness, Uncle Mack is from that generation where respect rules. A strict Jehovah's Witness he tries to see God in everything he does. A gentle giant, he and twelve siblings are the sons and daughters of Judge and Dossie Henderson Graham Malik's great-grandparents.

"I sure do miss those two," he says. "I couldn't keep a dollar in my pocket around them." Everyone smiles at the memory. "The police had better find some answers and quick, or I'm going to go looking myself!" yells Uncle Mack. Ms. Norma smiles. "Uncle Mack, don't you go running your month about things you know nothing about. Your just barely getting around yourself," she says.

"I get around good enough to kick some asses when I need to. Right, Kathy."

"Don't you two start please," says Kathy. Kathy is Jasmine's mom; she's where Jazz gets her looks and energy.

Ms. Norma's middle sister Catherine is sitting on the couch holding her son Dondi and daughter Michell. She's the quiet one in the family and both Dondi and Michell share this quality as well. Everyone is overwhelmed by this tragedy, including Uncle Bruce. Ms. Norma's only surviving brother who appears in the kitchen doorway. When he's upset, he cooks.

"Does anyone want anything to eat? I've prepared a small feast. Barbecue chicken, beef ribs, lamb, greens, corn bread, potato salad, macaroni and cheese, and several cakes and pies?" he says.

Jazz jumps up. "I'm starving!" she says then heads out the room, but Kathy stops her.

"Jazz, fix your mom something while you're in there please, and tell Bruce to wrap me up some of that lamb."

Slowly, everyone gets up and heads to the kitchen. Sakinah walks over to Malik. "Can I speak with you a minute, please?" she asks.

Malik follows Sakinah into his small office. "How are you holding up?" he asks.

"I'm holding on," says Sakinah.

"Yeah, me too, but I don't know how. I guess it's being taught not to cry when Allah takes his soul back. Believing that nothing happens without his permission and that in our babies being taken this way that there is a good in it somewhere, but I'm telling you, Sakinah, I'm struggling to see it. I went to the funeral home and washed and dressed them both. I told them you send your love and gave Eunique her baseball cap." Malik wipes his eyes,

Sakinah hugs him. "Where were you earlier? Before you went to the funeral home?" she asks. "I went to see Amin and Pup," he says.

"Why?"

"It's not important, besides, Amin was their godfather," says Malik.

"I know this, and yes, it is," Sakinah demands.

"No, it's not!" Malik shouts then walks away from her over to the window. The shades are closed.

"Malik, we have been together basically since seventh grade. I have never lied to you. I know you, Malik, I feel you. When you are happy, I feel you. When you are sad or angry or even in trouble, I feel that also no matter if you are miles away. I just hope you remember that." Sakinah opens the door then walks back in among the family. Malik stands there a moment then closes the door behind her. He walks over and takes a seat in the darkness of the room.

It's the next morning, Agent Oliver and Branch are entering the office of Captain Twyman. The captain sees them and gets up from his desk to greet them. "Good morning, gentlemen, what can I do for you?" he asks. Agent Branch is first into the office to greet him.

"Captain, thanks for taking time to see us." Branch extends his hand to the captain in a firm handshake. "As I said over the phone,

Agent Oliver and I are interested in the killing of the Davenport children."

The Captain motions for the agents to take a seat, then moves back around his desk to take his own. "Why would the FBI be interested in this case?" he asks.

"Because Agent Oliver and I believe that it could be the beginning of a series of murders, like what took place in Atlanta, back in seventy-nine through eighty-one."

Twyman leans back in his chair. "And why would you think that?"

"Agent Branch and myself have studied the similarities to other cases in the past. Such as, both of the children were shot in the head from close range, which indicated the shooter used rage as motivation or hate," says Oliver.

"There is no gang activity in that area. The children play in the streets. They wonder from house to house where they are welcomed and looked after as part of the community."

Agent Branch drives the point home further. "We believe that someone purposely drove through that area looking for someone to kill because it is upscale, with a mixture of both black and whites, something white supremacist are drastically against."

Captain Twyman gets out of his chair, comes around and sits on the front of his desk. "I see the logic in what you're saying. However, at this point we have no eye witnesses, no suspects, and no motives. The two detectives on the case Taylor and Brooks are attending the funerals of the two children and are not expected back here until late sometime this afternoon." Agent Branch stands then hands the Captain his card. "Here are the numbers where we can be reached. I'd appreciate it if you would have the detectives give us a call as soon as possible."

Agent Oliver opens the office door to leave but pauses and looks back at the captain. "We are not trying to take over this investigation in anyway, on the contrary, if possible and if need be, we would like to make available all our resources to you, to prevent another murder scandal like Atlanta," he says.

"I understand," says Captain Twyman. They all shake hands again. The agents turn then leave. Twyman goes back to his chair, flops down, blowing out a stream of air.

On the other side of town, there is not a cloud in the sky, as Malik, Sakinah, family, friends, and a host of spectators are standing around the grave site of the children. The Imam (spiritual leader) is standing between Kazi and Eunique, dressed in white pants, and a long white shirt. The body of the shirt coming almost down to his knees. The Imam is also wearing a beautiful burgundy and white Kufi (headdress). He turns to face the direction of the sacred Kaaba in Mecca (east), the direction from which all divine knowledge was born. Behind the Imam are three rows of men and women from the Islamic community all dressed in white. The Imam raises his hands up to his ears and says in a loud voice, "Allahu Akbar" (God is the greatest).

The Muslims in the rows behind him softly say the same, imitating his movement of raising the hands to their ears. The men then folding them under their navel. The women over their breast. The Imam begins the prayer. "Glory be to you oh Allah (God) and praises be to you and blessed is your name and exalted is your majesty and there is none worshipped but you." Without moving, his hands the Imam again says, "Allah Akbar!" (God is the greatest) and as before the three rows repeat what he has said without moving.

The Imam continues the prayer. "Oh, Allah (God), bless Muhammad and the followers of Muhammad, as you blessed Abrahim, for surely thy praise is magnified. Oh Allah (God) exalt Muhammad and the followers of Muhammad, as you did exalt Abrahim and the followers of Abrahim, for surely thy praise is magnified. The Imam again says, "Allahu Akbar." For the third time without moving and the row of Muslims repeat the same. The Imam again continues the prayer, "Oh, Allah (God), forgive those of us that are alive and those of us who are dead. Forgive those of us that are present and those of us who are absent. Those of us that are young and those of us that are adults—our males and our females. Oh, Allah (God), whomever of us you keep alive, let him live as a follower of Islam (submission) And whomever you cause to die, let him also die in a state of Islam." The Imam then says, "Allah Akbar" (God is the greatest) for the fourth time, then turning his head to the right he says: "As Salamu Alaikum Wa Rah Ma Tullah" (May peace be unto you and the mercy of God). Twice. He then turns his head to the left and says the same. The three rows repeat both what he has said and his movements.

The service being completed, Malik, Amin, Pup, and Nino another ex-Marine, step up front and lift Kazi off the platform, then lowers him into his grave, turning him to face Mecca. They do the same with Eunique. One by one family and friends collect two handfuls of dirt, then file by each of the graves throwing the dirt on top. Saying, "From the earth did we create you and into it shall we return you and from it shall we bring you out once more." Detectives Brooks and Taylor stand there in awe, fighting back their own tears.

CHAPTER 4

Reckless, skull, and three other white supremacist, Boomer, Joe-Earl, and J-Henry are sitting around in an old run-down trailer, drinking and getting high. The trailer park is on the outskirts of Mobile. Inside the trailer, clothing, food, empty containers, beer cans, and liquor bottles are thrown everywhere. They're all watching the news cast of the funeral of Kazi and Eunique. Boomer looks at Reckless and shakes his head. "I don't think you guys should have shot those kids. Hell, they were just babies," he says.

Boomer is six-foot-seven with a round face and stomach to match, little dark eyes and thin lips. Reckless glares at him. "It don't matter, Boomer. A nigger is a nigger and that's that!"

J-Henry shakes his head in agreement with Reckless. "Yea, those same nigger babies going to school with our children, integrating them to their filthy habits, like rap music and ways of doing things."

"Yea," says Joe-Earl, a short, blond-haired weasel of a man.

"If they wanna be safe, J-Henry, they should all just go on back to Af-fre-ka." Skull tosses a can at Boomer and misses.

"You're not going soft on us, are you?" he asks.

"Hell no! I'm just saying, killing those kids like that could cause a lot of problems."

"That's bullshit!" screams Skull. "No one ever saw me and Reckless. All those niggers and well-to-do white nigger lovers sleep late on Saturday morning anyway. They stay out all night at their fucking dinner parties and shit!" Reckless pulls out the gun he shot Kazi and Eunique with. "It don't matter, Joe-Earl." He flashes the automatic. "If they fucking wanna do something about it, I'm ready, man. FUCK THEM!" he shouts.

"Skull, are you sure no one seen you guys?" Boomer asks.

"I'm sure, Boom."

Skull gets up and stands beside Reckless as J-Henry, tall, skinny, and blind in one eye finishes off this beer, then crushes the can or the table. "Just the same," says Boomer, "Maybe you two better lay low for a few days until things quiet down." Reckless puts the gun back into his vest pocket then sits down. "I ain't running from nobody!" he says.

Joe-Earl jumps to his feet screaming, then walks over to Reckless and gets right up in his face. "You know, Reckless, you are crazy, you stupid son of a bitch! I agree with Boomer, you two should lay low. Just to make sure!"

Skull walks over and gently grabs Joe-Earl. "Hey, we cool with that, calm down. Right, buddy?" He slaps Reckless on the shoulder. "Right?"

Skull nudges Reckless. "Yeah, yeah we cool with that," says Reckless.

There is a sudden knock on the door. Everyone jumps! Boomer rushes to the door to look out the curtain. He then gives everyone the signal that it's okay. "It's Robyn and Cynthia," he says. Two black hookers that live in the trailer lot next door. Cynthia is the tallest of the two, at five-foot-nine, light-skinned, kinda homey looking with big eyes, and very wide hips. Robyn is light-skinned also, short, chunky, with a long face and high forehead. They both stand at the door dressed in short skirts that reveal a glimpse of their panty's. Their blouses are unbuttoned and tied at the waist. Boomer opens the door.

"Yeah," he says. Cynthia steps up front. "Hi, Boomer, me and Robyn was wandering if you boys wanted some company?"

Robyn steps to the side so Boomer can see her nipples through her top. "Hi, Boomer," she says with a fake smile.

As Boomer's eyes are riveted on her breast. "Hi, hi, Robyn," he says before hollering back into the trailer. "Y'all want some company?"

Reckless rushes to the door. "Shit, yeah, hey, girls," says Reckless, giving his best friendly smile. Cynthia and Robyn both say hi.

Reckless then pushes Boomer out the way. "Y'all come on in and make yourselves comfortable," he says. Cynthia allows Robyn to step in first. Then as she passes by eyeing Reckless, he grabs her on the ass. "Oh yeah, I like that," she says. She then rubs her hand up against his groin area.

"I know you do, honey," says Reckless. He grabs her behind again. "You look like you can take all of us at one time and love it."

"If the money is right, I'll see what I can do," she says.

Reckless closes the door, grabs Robyn, and takes her to the opposite end of the trailer.

Cynthia walks into where the others are and introduces herself. "Hi, boys, I'm Cynthia, who wants to party?" she asks as she unties the bottom of her blouse.

It's late evening, friends and family are all back at Malik's home eating and talking among themselves. Ms. Norma is sitting out on the patio with her cousins, nieces, nephews, sisters, and her mother's sister, Lois Lawrence. "Pat, my babies sure did look peaceful." Everyone nods in agreement. "Their father is a very strong man," says Pat.

"He prepared both of them for burial himself," she says. Kathy shakes her head.

"Honey, I don't know if I could have done all that myself. Mom and I were just talking about that."

"I'm with Kathy," Mary says.

"I know I couldn't. I think I would have been crying too much?"

"Me too," says Vodkie.

"I think I need to do more studying. I want that kind of strength and power, especially as a woman. Sometimes I think we as women are a bit too emotional. After all, we are the ones giving birth to both the babies and the Malik's of the world. To have that kind of understanding about how things work on this plane, I think it's great."

"Vodkie don't even go there," says Misha.

"Why not, Misha? Malik has already proven its safe," says Vodkie playfully as she sticks her tongue out at her big sister. Ms. Norma sits there playing with her glass. "I don't know whether or not it was the Marines or the religion of Islam that changed my son," she says. "But after both, he was never the same. He had this peaceful confidence about himself. A self-assurance kinda thing. He could be smiling one minute, and if he thought it was necessary, kill you the next. Then sit down like nothing happened. I remember when he came home from boot camp and for the first few months afterward, he would get into fights out in the streets, then come home covered in blood. I would jump up screaming, thinking he was injured and he would say: 'No, Mom, it's someone else's blood.' Then he'd run upstairs, change clothes, then go right back out like nothing happened."

Mary puts her hand up to her mouth. "Oh my God!" she says.

"Yeah, girl, it was crazy. It happened so regularly that I stopped even asking. Pat will tell you."

"I remember one night around twelve thirty," says Pat. "I was talking to Norma on the phone when he came in like that."

"Girl, my son had blood covering him from head to toe. Splattered all on his face, in his hair. He had on a white shirt with blue pin strips, and it looked as though he was leaking blood!" says Ms. Norma. "I heard her scream over the phone and ask him are you bleeding. I couldn't hear what he said, but when Norma got back on the phone she said, 'Girl, Malik just came in covered in blood. The Marines have just messed him up!'" says Pat.

Vodkie, Misha and the others burst out laughing. "That was the last time I seen him like that," says Ms. Norma. "Later he told me he had fought out at the skating ring. Some guy name Terry Gilmore. You all know policeman Gilmore."

Everyone implies that they do. "Well, his son. In fact, Malik says that when the ambulance was pulling up for Terry so was officer Gilmore that he was the first police car at the scene."

"Why were they fighting?" Misha asks. "Malik says that some girl name Joan Palmer was going with Terry, but lied and told him Malik tried to have sex with her. Not knowing this, Malik pulled over for him one night, a few days later, and when he got out the car to see what the guy wanted, Terry threatened Malik and verbally abused him in front of the people in Terry's car, basically just showing off for Joan, who was in the car also, because he knew Malik had been celebrating heavily.

"When they saw each other at the skating ring months later, after Malik returned home, the same guy skated over to Malik while he was sitting talking to Boo Carter and rolled right over the tip of Malik's shoe. He then skated back onto the floor backward, laughing at Malik."

"Did Malik cut him or something?" Mary asks.

"We all know how good he and his boys are with knives," says Misha.

"No, he said he went outside and put on Nationwide's gym shoes, gave Christin Cameron his hat and jewelry to hold, then walked back inside. Terry had already taken his skates off by that time and was waiting."

"I think I remember hearing about that," says Vodkie.

"But why did they call the ambulance, terry is twice Malik's size."

"I guess the owners thought it was needed. Malik says he didn't hit Terry nowhere below the neck. He says Terry was bigger and stronger, but he remembered what his close combat drill instructor told him on Paris Island: 'If you scramble the computer room (The Brain) your opponent's strength, arms, legs, and hands won't work.'"

Misha and the others burst out laughing again. Auntie Lois throws her hands up and looks at the sky. "Girl, what you gonna do with that boy?" she says. "I wish his grandmother, my sister was here to see how much he has grown. She loved that boy more than anything."

"Auntie Lois, how long has she been gone now?" asks Vodkie.

"Since 1978, she died very young," says Lois, who then stands and stretches. "I think I'm going to lie down for a while," she says before heading toward the house. The laughter dies down as Ms. Norma continues, and as other family members gather around to listen in on what's being said.

"After he became a Sunni Muslim, Malik began to study more. I mean everything. Science, religion, politics, philosophy, African history, cause and effect, everything. He told me one day, he said, 'Mom, I feel sorry for a lot of people, because they just don't know. It's like Jesus said when they put Him on the Cross. Forgive them, Lord, for they know not what they do.' I just sat and looked at him," says Ms. Norma. FeeFee stands up to go inside. "Malik is a real man, unlike his father. He'll never know the man he gave life too," she says. Her sister Poo stands up to leave with her. "That's his loss, FeeFee!"

"That's what I said, Poo."

"I'd give my life for my sons," says Ms. Norma, as everyone else sits back quietly lost in their own thoughts.

Malik is in the kitchen talking with Nino, Pup, and Amin. While Sakinah is busy preparing food on a tray along with glasses of ice tea to take outside. Sakinah is wearing an Ashanti cloth dress, with head wrap. Kazi's favorite. Every time she wore it he would say: "Ummi (Mother) you look like a queen." She glances at Malik out the corner of her eye, as Nino walks over to her.

"Sakinah, how you doing sister? Can I help you with that?" he asks.

Nino is not just an ex-Marine, he's also Malik's cousin. People sometimes mistake him for Tito Jackson. "I'm hanging in there, Nino," she says.

Amin walks over. "You keep on doing that. Nothing will change what's been done, but as time passes, it can get a little easier to make it through the next day."

Sakinah smiles. "Thank you, Amin."

Pup puts his arm around Malik. "She's got this guy to lean on. She'll be just fine," he says.

Malik and Sakinah look directly at each other. "I honestly don't know what I would have done without him these last few days," she says before picking up the tray with the food and drinks, then turning to head outside. Pup with his arm still round Malik squeezes him. "That's a hell of a woman you got there bro."

"I know," says Malik. Amin learns back on the counter.

"Yeah, the creator is something else man, sometimes he takes when he gives and sometimes he gives when he takes. You just have to have the wisdom to know which one of these states you're in?"

Malik and Amin bump fists together. "I feel you, bro," says Malik.

"Still nothing from the cops?" Nino asks.

"Nothing, Nino, but I have people with their ears open."

"I know, Amin and Pup told me. Everybody mad about this shit gee, count me in on whatever, whenever, however!" says Nino. They all pick up their glasses of tea in a toast. As godfather Amin is the toast master. "To the little lion cub and the princess. Forever loved!"

They all click glasses in unison. "Forever loved!"

Detective Taylor and Brooks are entering the police station looking withdrawn, having returned from the funeral and a late lunch where neither one was particularly hungry. They exchange greetings with other detectives and officers, as they make their way to Captain Twyman's office. Twyman is sitting at his desk reading reports when they knock then enter his office. He looks up, taking off his glasses. "How did it go?" he asks.

Brooks flops down in a chair then loosens up his tie. "It was beautiful. I've never been to a Muslim funeral before," he says.

"Yeah," says Taylor.

"Nobody really cried. I mean none of the people who believe in the Islamic faith. Tracy and I asked one of the guys after the funeral why and he said that the Muslim faith teaches them that nothing happens without the permission of God, Allah, and that the day that every soul will leave the earth and how, is written in a divine book. There is nothing anyone can do about it."

"Yeah," says Brooks. "He said that Islam means (Submission) and that Muslims are those who submit to God's will. Chief, you should have seen it!" Brooks is animated.

"They dressed the children in plain white cloth and buried them lying on their right sides facing the building Abraham and his son Ishmael built," says Taylor.

"Hell, I never knew Abraham built a house." Twyman snaps back to the present. "How's the investigation coming along. Oh, before I forget." He hands Taylor the card from Oliver and Branch. "Two FBI agents came by the station this morning wanting to talk with whoever was directly handling the Davenport murders. I told them I would give you this."

Brooks sits up in his chair. "Why would the FBI want that info?" he asks. "Because they believe that the murders may be race related," says Twyman. "Something like what took place back in Atlanta in seventy-nine through eighty-one, when all those black children were killed."

Taylor and Brooks glance at each other. The captain notices. "What's up?" he asks.

Taylor clears his throat. "Sir, we went to talk with Ms. Stanton and her son, Kevin, he was a good friend of the Davenport's children. His mother believed Kevin had seen the shootings because he was afraid. He had hid in his closet and wouldn't talk to anyone. Anyways, I spoke with him and he said he seen the shooting."

"What!" says Twyman, jumping out of his seat then racing around to the front of his desk.

"Who have you told this to?" he asks.

"No one, Tracy and I thought it would be best that we wait until after the funeral," says Brooks. "I suggested to Steve that he ask Ms. Stanton to keep things quiet and to keep Kevin home until then also."

Twyman looks over to Taylor. "What did Kevin say?" he asks.

"He said he seen two white bald head guys roll up behind the children. He heard a pop, the girl scream, another pop, and the car drove off real fast," says Taylor.

"Did he get a good look at the guys or the car?" asks Twyman.

"He just said that the guys were white and bald. But he did get a good look at the car. He said it was a blue racing car with the engine sticking out the front, white strips on the side, with a skull painted on the back."

Twyman goes back around behind his desk, puts his glasses back on, then pulls a folder out of his desk drawer. "Let's get an APB out on the car with that description and get a sketch artist over to the Stanton's house to see if Kevin can help draw a clear picture for ID purposes."

Taylor stands up, smoothing out his slacks. "I'll call Ms. Stanton and see if we can set up something for early tomorrow morning," he says.

"Chief." Brooks also stands up. "I think maybe I should also call the Davenports and let them know that we have a lead in the case and see if I can meet with them tomorrow also," he says.

"I think that's a good idea," says the captain. "Eventually they will find out from Ms. Stanton. She feels just awful," says Taylor.

"She told me when I spoke to her that she doesn't want the Davenports thinking she was hiding something. Oh, and one more thing. What should Tracy and I do about the FBI agents?"

"Play it any way you want," says Twyman.

"I think we should talk with Kevin, the Davenports and everyone in the neighborhood about this car first, then the agents." Brooks suggests.

"That's fine with me," says the chief.

Taylor walks on out the door, Brooks follows stopping just inside the door. "Who knows, they may already have a file on these guys?"

"You two go home and get some rest, something tells me after today there is not going to be much of that for a while," says Twyman.

The captain closes the door then sits back down looking at the folders on his desk. He presses the button on his phone. "Charlott, is Lieutenant Jackson back yet?"

"I'm not sure, sir, you want me to page him?" she asks.

"Yes, see if he's around and tell him to come to my office."

"Yes, sir." The captain's secretary pages the Lieutenant. Minutes later, he arrives and steps into the captain's office.

"What's up chief?" he asks.

"Steve and Tracy just left, they spoke with a neighbor's son who said he seen two white men with bald heads shoot the Davenport children then drive away in a blue racing car with white strips."

"What!" says Jackson, clearly blown away; he stumbles back into one of the chairs against the wall.

"Yes," says the captain.

"What do you want to do?" Jackson asks.

Twyman takes a deep breath. "Tomorrow Steve and Tracy are going to inform the Davenports and try to get a sketch from the neighbor's son on the car. I think you know what the potential is for a race riot once this information goes public."

"I'm following you," says Jackson.

"So we need to get some people out there active in the black communities to help us keep the peace."

"I can call some of the ministers at the different churches and ask for their help," Jackson suggests.

"Okay, and let's get prepared to deal with the college students, the high school, and junior high levels."

"I'll start making some calls," says Jackson as he stands to leave. "You know, Chief, it's very possible that we may not be able to contain this. A lot of people are very upset about the murder of those children. Once this is out, that white skinheads are responsible, yet again, there might be some random killing of white kids?" Jackson suggests.

"This is the same thing the sheriff said down there is Jasper, Texas, when those three white boys kidnapped James Byrd, beat him, then tied him by his ankles to their pickup truck, then drug him for three miles," says Jackson.

"I know, they're animals."

"Chief, black people are about fed up with that kinda thing." Jackson looks at the captain for a minute then closes the door.

It's late evening at the Davenports. Malik, Sakinah, Hugh Lamont, and Ms. Norma are the only ones left at the house. Ms. Norma is laying on the couch in the living room. Malik enters the room from the kitchen where Hugh and Sakinah are still sitting. Malik looks very tired. "Mom, are you okay?"

"I'm just resting. What about you, how are you doing?" she asks.

"I'm okay." Silence. "I sure do miss them," says Malik.

"I know, baby, I know, I miss them too." Ms. Norma reaches for Malik and pulls him to her chest. She strokes his face and head. "It's going to get easier, baby. Just hold on," she says.

Back in the kitchen, Hugh Lamont is talking to Sakinah. "What's up with Malik?" he asks. Sakinah gives him a confused look.

"What do you mean?"

"I mean, all day he's been whispering and talking with those ex-Marine friends of his. And the one tall guy."

"Pup?" she asks.

"Yes, him. He just kept looking at me all day," says Hugh.

"As you know Amin was Kazi and Eunique's godfather. Pup, Nino, Terrible T, Pasqually, Monk, Ant-Head, and Cuddy are very loyal to each other and Malik. Malik says that there is nothing like the bond of service men, especially the Marines. Malik never turned his back on any of them after he stared making a lot of money. He helped them all, they love him. You should try to get along with them, they are all good guys. They have always treated me with respect," says Sakinah.

"I just feel like they are up to something," says Hugh.

"That may be, but it's none of your business!"

"I'm just looking out for you," Hugh says. "I can look out for myself and as I recall, I've been looking out for you. Let's not forget that Malik did not even want you in this house Hugh Lamont after you slept with his old girlfriends, even after they told you they had been with him."

Hugh jumps up then goes to the refrigerator, snatching the door open. "I don't want to hear this!" he shouts.

"And when he was struggling and you had money to help, you turned your back and helped everyone else except him," says Sakinah.

"Malik has always tried to tell me what to do." Hugh takes a swallow of his cola.

"You know what your problems are?" Sakinah asks.

"What?" Hugh asks.

"For one, you don't know the difference between being told what to do and being given sound advice."

"Yes, I do!" snaps Hugh Lamont before taking his seat back at the kitchen counter.

"No, you don't! When you came into that money, everyone had an idea of how you should spend it. You brought cars, jeeps, motorcycles, and furnished apartments and homes for the sons and the daughter of that woman your father had living with him. But Malik couldn't borrow money for an attorney to deal with the legal problems he was battling because you said he was trying to tell you what to do? You lied to friends and to family members, having them believing that you were helping him, sending money, talking with lawyers on his behalf while the truth was very different. You gave no serious effort. It was all a game to you, because you are a coward."

"Malik threatened to kill me!" shouts Hugh Lamont.

"I don't blame him, I probably would have killed you myself if I were him, after he practically raised you. It's funny you mentioned Malik's alleged threat to kill you because Malik spoke to the lawyer, Danny O'Brian, the one you said you would give the twenty-five grand to on his behalf, and he said you changed your mind, that you would not be writing him a check because you feared if Malik was in a room with you, he'd harm you, and when Aunt Lois called you, telling you to help Malik, you told her the same thing, in spite of her repeatedly saying that wasn't true, and reminding you of all Malik done for you. You are a great liar…just like your Dad, Hugh Collins. He told lies about Malik to Tammy Gamble and she told Malik because she knew it wasn't true. After Malik called your father and asked him about what he was saying, your father went uptown and told lies to the prosecutor for protection. I guess he didn't feel safe either huh, especially after lying on someone you both know will put his foot in your ass. When your father left our mom who you think sent money for you to eat? Who purchased your school clothes. Including your first football gear? Who brought you toys for Christmas? Who came to pick you up, and take you out to eat and ride around? I'll tell you who, Malik. Malik believes that you're jealous of him and that you would love to see him fail or for something to happen to him," says Sakinah.

"That's not true!" Hugh screams again.

"Malik believes it is."

"I don't care what Malik believes."

Sakinah gets up, closes the blinds to the patio, then comes back and sits right in front of Hugh. "Even when our own mother was sick and diagnosed a diabetic, you left her in that old house with no air-conditioning for years, while your fathers people lived in a brand-new home you paid for even after your father died. You would come home and visit, riding around with your football friends and oftentimes, Mom never even knew you had been there until she bumped into someone on the streets who had either seen you there or been with you. Imagine her surprise."

"That's a lie!" says Hugh.

"You slandered her character among your friends and your play brothers and sisters, because she asked you for help. You left her begging for every dime you gave her while you gave to all your friends freely. For almost twenty years, she didn't have your phone number while she lived practically homeless even after having a stroke. Why didn't you buy her a house? Because you didn't give a damn! What did Kerry do to you except help raise you and protect you! Did he threaten you too? Or did he also try to tell you what to do? In all these years and all that money that went through your hands, the job at ESPN, ETC, you sent Kerry four hundred dollars once. You gave Malik a thousand dollars once, and even though you flew out to LA monthly, tricking with the girls you knew out there, you never went to see Kerry, not once. You paid for your ex-high school and college football uniforms for ten years, you paid for a new high school score board, swings for the park, but nothing for mom and you were her only source of income. You'll do anything to shine in outsiders' eyes." Sakinah slaps him. "And don't raise your voice in my home."

Hugh sits there with his head down staring at his feet, Malik walks into the kitchen. "Baby, I put Mom in the guest bedroom. She was too tired to drive home," he says. Malik then stands there looking at Hugh then Sakinah, sensing something has been going on. Sakinah gets up, placing the remainder of her drink in the refrigerator.

"That's fine, I was going to ask her to stay anyway so that she can help me go through the children's things tomorrow, Inshallah."

"You about ready for bed?" Malik ask.

"Very much so," she says. "Let's go."

Malik reaches out his hand, Sakinah takes it. He turns back to Hugh. "You leaving or staying?" he asks.

"I'm leaving," says Hugh.

"Make sure you set the alarm and lock the door on your way out," says Malik.

"I will." Sakinah walks by Hugh and stops.

"Good night," she says. Hugh looks at her.

"Good night." Malik and Sakinah head upstairs. Once inside their bedroom they begin to undress. Malik heads for the bathroom. "I think I'm going to take a shower," he says before stepping inside it to adjust the water temperature.

Malik undresses then steps into the shower allowing the water to run over his head and shoulders. Moments later, Sakinah walks in and opens the shower door.

"Move over," she says.

"Anything for you," says Malik. She steps in and they embrace. Malik takes the shower sponge, lathers it up, then begins washing Sakinah's back and shoulders, kissing her lightly on the back of her neck and behind her ears. "I love you," Malik whispers; Sakinah begins to cry.

Thirty minutes later, shower completed and Sakinah is sitting in front of her vanity mirror drying her hair. Malik is at the sink brushing his teeth. Sakinah pauses to look at her husband. "They looked really beautiful today all dressed in white. You done good."

"Thanks, you helped to keep everyone's head up today. They felt better because of you," says Malik.

"I get my strength from you and Allah. You've taught me a lot over the years," Sakinah says. "I've learned from you as well."

Malik rinses his mouth out then puts his toothbrush up. He moves over to his side of the bed, pulling the covers back then sits down to gaze at his wife. "You're so beautiful," he says.

Sakinah smiles. "Thank you."

She finishes wrapping her hair, cleans the countertop off, before coming over to her side of the bed, sliding under the covers then up under her husband. Malik reaches to turn the lights off before embracing Sakinah fully, wrapping her in a strong embrace. Kissing her lightly over her lips then her face.

"I want you to know, Sakinah, that the word *love* never meant anything to me without you. And through that love and because of it, you gave me a son that was the pride and joy of his father, and a daughter who melts my heart at the thought of her."

Tears roll down both their faces as Malik continues, "I know that Allah tests us with what we love most. 'Cause for sure, the only thing that comes close to matching the love I have for you is the love I have for Kazi and Eunique. We did good though baby, in those eleven short years we raised two individuals whose love and devotion to family and each other." Malik struggles to hold back his tears. "Was truly something to marvel at. I cannot wait to see them both again."

Sakinah props herself up on one elbow leaning over to kiss Malik's tears away before resting her head on his chest again. "Me too," she says. Malik pulls the covers up over Sakinah's shoulders as he holds her. Wondering what's to come of her if something happens to him.

CHAPTER 5

It's the next morning, Ms. Norma is answering a knock at the door. It's Detective Brooks. "May I help you?" she asks.

"Hi, how are you doing this morning, Mrs. Davenport?"

"Fine."

"I was wondering if your son was home?" he asks.

"Yes, he is."

"If possible, may I speak to him? It's important," says the detective.

Ms. Norma looks at him for a moment. "Sure, come on in, I'll see if he is awake." Ms. Norma steps back so that Brooks can enter. "Have a seat, I'll send him right down," she says.

"Thank you," says Brooks as he walks into the den.

Ms. Norma goes upstairs and knocks lightly on Malik's bedroom door. "Malik, you awake?" she asks.

"Come on in, Mom," says Malik.

Ms. Norma walks into the bedroom. "Good morning, you two. How did you sleep?" she asks. "Sound, but Malik snored all night," says Sakinah.

Malik looks over at her. "I only do that when I'm extremely tired," he says.

Ms. Norma smiles at them both. "Detective Brooks is downstairs, he says he wants to speak with you."

"Oh yeah," says Malik. Sakinah looks over at him. "I wonder what he wants?" she asks.

"Mom, tell him I'll be down in a few minutes," Malik says.

"Okay, you two want some breakfast?"

Sakinah stretches. "I'm not really hungry. I think I'll come down and try a bowl of cereal," she says.

"I'm okay, Mom," says Malik.

"All right." Ms. Norma walks out of the room, down the stairs, and into the den where the detective is sitting. "Malik said that he will be down shortly," she says.

"Thank you again. I'm sorry about what happened to your grandchildren," Brooks says.

"Thank you. Would you like some breakfast, a glass of juice, tea, or coffee?" Ms. Norma asks.

"A cup of coffee would be nice," says Brooks.

"How do you drink your coffee?" asks Ms. Norma.

"Black, no cream, two scoops of sugar," says Detective Brooks.

"Coming up," says Ms. Norma before heading into the kitchen to prepare the coffee.

Back upstairs, Malik is getting dressed while Sakinah is in the shower. Malik walks over to the door. "Do you want to sit in on this?" he asks.

Sakinah yells over the running water. "If you want me to?"

"It's entirely up to you," Malik replies.

"I'll get dressed and come down," she says.

"Okay." Malik tucks his shirt into his pants, slips on his shoes then heads down the steps and into the living room where Brooks is waiting. Brooks stands up extending his hand. "Good morning, Mr. Davenport."

Malik shakes his hand. "How are you, Detective?"

"It's too early to tell yet," says Brooks with a smile.

"Have a seat," Malik says.

Ms. Norma walks in with a tray of coffee, cheese Danish, and a glass of orange juice for Malik. "Here you are," she says, placing the tray on the table.

Brooks reaches for his cup then takes a sip. "Delicious! Thank you," he says.

"Thanks, Mom," says Malik.

Ms. Norma smiles then turns to leave the room. "I'll be in the kitchen if you need anything," she says. Malik waits until she leaves the room then turns back to Brooks. "What can I help you with Detective?" He asks. Brooks looks nervous. He sits his coffee down. "Mr. Davenport, we know who shot your children," he says.

"WHO!" Malik snaps.

"Ms. Stanton's son says that he seen two bald white men drive up behind them in a blue racing car, shoot them both, then drive off. He was afraid, so he hid in his closet."

Malik stands then paces to the fireplace and back, wiping his hand over his head. Visibly shaken. "You mean two white assholes murdered my children just for the hell of it? And little Kevin saw it? I can't believe this shit!" says Malik, trembling, fighting to remain calm.

Sakinah walks in, realizing instantly that Malik is upset. "You can't believe what, baby?" she asks.

Malik looks at her, wondering whether or not to inform her. "Tell her what you told me, Detective," he says.

Sakinah looks at Brooks. "Ms. Stanton's son saw two bald white men shoot your children."

Malik studies her reaction. "Right now, he's with a sketch artist at his home trying to put together a picture of the car," says Brooks.

Sakinah walks over and sits down in the chair next to the fireplace. "You know, Detective, as a child, I would listen to my mother and grandmother talk about the racism they seen and experienced here in the south. My paternal grandmother was born in 1909. Can you imagine all the horror she seen, Mr. Brooks?" Sakinah stares at him, willing her tears not to fall.

"Yes, I can, Mrs. Davenport. I too have similar horror stories to tell as does my family members."

"When does it end?" Sakinah asks to no one in particular. "How many people have to die for having or being something they have no control over?" she asks.

Malik looks at Brooks, but before he can respond, Sakinah continues almost unconsciously. "No one has gone out and killed whites for being white. And these people, some of them, not all, have historically committed acts which deserve nothing short of death."

Malik walks over and places his hand on his wife's shoulder. "And so they shall have it!" he says.

"Mr. and Mrs. Davenport, I want you both to know that I am just as out raged over this as you are." Brooks plays with his hands; he doesn't know what else to say.

Sakinah gets up, looks at him then heads out the room. "You couldn't possibly be!" she says.

Malik watches her leave then takes her seat. "You know, Detective Brooks, in this country, whites have always looked out for each other. Even the police. When white supremacist were lynching, beating, raping, and bombing black homes and churches, whites in power, the US Supreme Court Justices, the presidents, Congress, local judges, both federal and state. The all-white juries, federal and state law enforcement, all played their role in supporting those whites who had done those crimes. They broke all the rules, ignored the laws. They had no problem using their positions to perpetuate white dominance, by trying to instill fear in blacks, Asians, Hispanics, and other people of color. In my lifetime no one has ever gone after white supremacist, men, women, or children in direct response to what they have done to the families of others. Sure, you have these quasi pro black militants walking around with their guns on display, trying to recruit others to do what they should be doing themselves.

"Since the birth of the Panthers in the sixties, up until now, none of these groups have used those weapons to any significant degree, just their mouths. When I was in Nam, I had orders to kill. We killed some women and children because they supported the troops we were fighting against."

Brooks nods his head in agreement. Malik continues. "I believe it's necessary when you do an operation, to eliminate the entire cancer otherwise, it will only regenerate and spread to other healthy parts of the body."

Malik gets up then moves over and sits on the coffee table in front of Detective Brooks. "That's what has happened here in this country, Detective. The cancer has been allowed to spread, primarily because the wrong cure has been used to fight it. Detective do you believe that it's possible to make a moral plea to the immoral?" Malik asks.

"I've never really thought about it," says Brooks nervously.

"Think about it this way then. Did your grandfather or grandmother ever pick up a stick or a brick and knock those people who were murdering them, and beating them, upside the head?"

"I don't think so, my grandparents were peaceful, God-fearing people," says Brooks.

"God-fearing or white-fearing, Detective? Because millions of our nation today foolishly believe God is white, a white man with blond hair and blue eyes. Sadly they are the majority in this country, and their stupidity is what has boxed us all in."

Brooks doesn't respond.

"Did your grandparents or your own parents ever tell you when you were a kid, 'If somebody hits you, you hit them back?' Malik asks. Do you remember being told that, Detective?"

"Yes, I believe most black children were told that by their parents," says Brooks

"And I assume you were raised up in a mostly black community or neighborhood?"

"That's correct," Brooks agrees hesitantly, not knowing where Malik is heading with this.

"So I guess what your parents were actually telling you and all the other black children, is that they should fight their own with anything they get their hands on. But when they are attacked and murdered by whites because of their skin color or their request of fair treatment in America, they should pray? Put up no resistance? Sing we shall overcome someday? Or some other land mark submissive slave tune that puts off doing what needs to be done today for some possible day in the distant future? Or leave it in the hands of the Lord who has historically allowed men to fight their own battles. He may create the causes for victory. But men must make a stand! Every time we have found a way to pull ourselves up, these people have placed road blocks in our way to keep us down, SLAVE CODES, BLACK CODES, JIM CROW, RED LINING, TERROR, AND

LYNCHING CAMPAINS." Again Brooks is speechless; he sits back on the couch.

They burned our homes, businesses, and all black towns and communities to the ground—like in Tulsa, Oklahoma; Rosewood, Florida; and many other locations across the country—all because some silly white woman lied saying a black had looked at her, spoken to her, or whistled at her. Thousands lost their lives, and everything they owned went up in smokes! The federal government, the all-white racist government, supplied the airplanes that dropped the bombs on the black wall street—blowing it to pieces, killing thousands of men, women, and children who had done nothing wrong, broken no laws. Becoming even more sinister, they devised a diabolical plot to halt black independence of whites by creating what they called "urban city planning" across the country. Almost every black community in America was disassembled, and the people were made to leave their homes, schools, and businesses behind to make room for roads, highways, and bridges. Excuse my language, but this racist white man, this greedy sinister white man, is a motherfucker! This is the same white man as a priest, a man of God, allegedly representing God on Earth across the globe who is routinely a pedophile. This is the same racist white man that created Boy Scouts of America in 1910 so that he could have an unlimited supply of young boys to molest. This racist white man routinely rapes and molests his own sons and daughters. It's time for him to go! He values nothing except his own wants and needs, and those who have been taught and trained to worship his image have taken on his vicious disregard for life.

"Could this be why so many black men and women across the country today, have no conscience regarding killing their own people for little or nothing, Mr. Brooks? Gunning each other down for little or nothing? But this white enemy who has declared open war on people of color and butchered them for hundreds of years in unspeakable ways, to him and his kind, you turn the other cheek. Offering love, forgiveness, and peace! I almost threw up when ex-Alabama governor George Wallace died and weak black men were shown carrying his coffin. Here is a racist responsible for the death and injuries of thousands of black men, women, and children. For years he used his position to terrorize blacks in the south, and yet upon his death these weak Southern Baptist Knee grows stampeded to carry his coffin. 'We forgive him,' they said. Christianity taught by whites around the world has been corrupted, and it has made Black men who follow it, BITCHES."

"I see your point, Mr. Davenport," says Brooks.

Malik stands then walks to the fire place again picking up his glass. "Do you? Really? We will see. Is there anything else, Detective?" Malik asks.

"Oh, no, not at the moment," says Brooks before standing as Malik walks past him heading toward the front door. Malik opens the door then turns to face the detective. "When you find these people responsible for murdering my children, I want to be the first to know," he says.

"I can't allow you to take matters into your own hands, Mr. Davenport," says Brooks.

"I don't expect you to, that would go against how you were raised to respond to racism," says Malik, stepping aside to allow the detective to pass through the door, before slamming it behind him! Across the street Detective Taylor is in the living room at the Stanton home with Kevin and a very pretty young sketch artist named Sissy, who has a pair of the biggest brightest eyes, you ever want to see. Lenora, Detective Taylor and Gen are sitting quietly as Sissy points to her drawing.

"Kevin, were the strips on the side of the car wide like this or smaller?" she asks.

"Wide like that." Kevin points at the second set of strips.

"Okay, Kevin, where was the skull at?"

Kevin points to the back of the car on the drawing.

"Back here?" asks Sissy. "Was it at the very back of the car, on the side, or on the trunk?"

"It was on the side at the back," says Kevin.

"Like this?" Sissy draws the skull back by the back side blinker.

"Yes, like that," says Kevin, nodding his head.

"Did it have anything on it, any paint or design?"

"It had red eyes."

Sissy colors the eyes red on the sketch. "Where the eyes like this?" she asks.

"Yes."

"Okay, Kevin, what about the big engine you seen, what did it look like?"

Before Kevin can answer, there is a knock at the door. It's Detective Brooks. Gen goes to the door and opens it. "Hello, Detective. Come on in," she says.

Brooks walks inside. "How are you doing, Ms. Woodson?" he asks.

"I asked you to call me Gen. I'm fine," she says.

"Okay then, is Detective Taylor still here?" Brooks asks.

"Yes, he's in the living room, come in."

Gen closes the door then leads Brooks into the living room where Taylor sees him and motions for Brooks to step back out the room. "How did it go with the Davenports?" he asks.

"As well as could be expected. The Davenport's have a better understanding of the world and events in it than most people. Because of it, I believe there is very little they can't deal with," says Brooks. Taylor nod in agreement. "How are things coming here?" Brooks asks.

"Sissy is almost done. Little Kevin is very intelligent for a nine-year-old." Brooks looks into the room at Lenora holding Kevin on her lap. "His mother has a good relationship with him. I wonder where his father is?" Taylor raises and drops his shoulders. "I don't know, neither one of them has mentioned him."

Brooks continues looking at the two of them. "She's very pretty and very sincere. Whatever happened I know he has nothing but regrets now."

"I can imagine," says Taylor.

Sissy stands then walks over with a completed sketch of the car. "This is the vehicle we are looking for. Kevin has a pretty good memory for a child, and he is certain that this is just like the car he seen," she says.

Taylor looks closely at the drawing. "Okay, well we need to head on back to the station so that we can get an APB out on this."

"Just let me get the rest of my things," says Sissy.

She walks back into the living room, stooping down as she places paper and colored pencils back into her carrying bag. She closes it then stops in front of Kevin who is still sitting on his moms lap. "Kevin, may I have a hug?" she asks.

Kevin looks up at his mother; she smiles, nodding her approval. "Yes," he says.

Sissy then hugs Kevin and kisses him. "You're a very brave little man. I know your mom is very proud of you."

Lenora squeezes him. "I sure am," she says. Kevin laughs. Detective Taylor steps back into the room. "Ms. Stanton we want to thank you both for your help and patience. We know this has been difficult for you," he says.

Lenora stands with Kevin. "It's been difficult for everyone. Is it all right for us to visit and talk with Malik and Sakinah now? Malik is like a father to Kevin."

"Sure, Detective Brooks was just there. I'm sure they too are very grateful for the help Kevin has provided." Brooks ducks into the room.

"Steve, we need to be going!" he says. "I'm right behind you," says Taylor before turning back to Lenora. "Thanks again." He then shakes hands with Kevin. "You take care of your mom."

"I will," Kevin says.

Brooks, Taylor, and Sissy make their way out to the car, Brooks is driving. He puts the key into the ignition then pauses to glance at Steve and Sissy. "I believe all hell is about to break loose," he says. Sissy looks at him puzzled.

"Why do you say that?" she asks.

"Because the marines have landed." Sissy and Steve look at Brooks then each other as Detective Brooks starts the car then pulls off. Back at Malik's home.

Ms. Norma is walking into the living room where Malik is sitting. She's trying to put on a brave face for her son, but she is devastated over the loss of her grandchildren. She sits next to him and takes his hand. "You know, son, I didn't even know that I was pregnant with you until you popped out two and a half months premature. Your granny, your aunties and your uncle Bruce used to carry you around on this little pillow. The doctor didn't really expect you to live. We had to buy a special formulated milk for you that cost a dollar and sixty-two cents a can. Many days, your father and I got into arguments and fights over him talking your milk money and spending it on beer and liquor. My mom would sing to you and rock you for hours. She'd say, 'Norma, ain't nothing going to happen to this boy, he's a fighter.' And she was right."

Malik stares off into the distance. "You would get really sick sometimes, but you kept on growing. Do you remember the nick name your granny gave you?" Malik doesn't answer. "She called you Pappi because you were so alert and grown." Ms. Norma smiles at the memories. "Even when you were only three, you would walk around trying to police and protect the family or anyone hurt or sick, even animals. I remember one day we were all in the park cooking and celebrating and your brother Kerry was in this swing just swinging away. This older bigger kid came over and made Kerry get out the swing. You saw him then ran over and hit him until he got out the swing. You then called Kerry back over and said, 'Here you go, Kerry, swing.' You were three and Kerry was four. Sometimes your Aunt Pat's boyfriend would make her cry and you would come over and place her head on your chest, and say, 'Don't cry.' You've always protected other people and fought their battles. You were born into it. Both your grandmothers thought you were special, and gave you a lot of love."

Malik places his other hand on top of hers. "I know, Mom. I think of my grannies every single day."

"I heard what that detective said and I also heard what you said. I raised you to fight back also, no matter who it is. If anyone hits you, you should hit them back!" Mother and son look directly at each other for a moment. No words needing to be spoken. Ms. Norma reaches over and kisses him, before standing up and walking out the room. Malik sits there a while longer somewhat relieved that his mother senses what's to come.

It's early morning; Robyn is coming out of the trailer with Reckless hanging and feeling all over her. He's drunk, carrying a half-empty bottle of Jack Daniels. "Damn, baby! Ain't you had enough yet?" she asks.

"Do it look like I had enough?" Reckless stops and thrusts his pelvic out so Robyn can see he's aroused. Cynthia and Skull come out the room behind them. "It's sure nice of you to give us a ride over my girlfriend Harriet's house," says Cynthia.

"It's no problem, darling. I need to get out for a while, I can't stand to be cooped up too long. I'm a free spirit," says Skull.

As they approach the car, Cynthia marvels at it. "Is this your car?" she asks.

"Yep, I fixed it up and painted it myself," says Skull before taking her to the backside of the car.

"Lookie here." He shows her the skull on the side with the red eyes. Cynthia looks at it, then at him as they moved around to the driver and passenger sides of the car.

"Why do they call you Skull?" she asks.

They're interrupted by Robyn climbing in with Reckless following right behind her. Skull and Cynthia then get in closing the door. Skull starts the car and they shoot out the lot. He looks over at Cynthia sensing she's enjoying the ride. "They call me that because when I was younger I used to do a lot of crazy shit and people would say I must be clean out of my skull. So everyone just started calling me that." Reckless slaps him on the back of his head.

"Yeah, he's a crazy son of a bitch all right."

Skull recoils, grabs his neck, then continues talking to Cynthia. "Are you girls originally from Mobile?" he asks.

Robyn leans over the front seat. "I was born and raised in Helena, Arkansas, but I lived in Ohio for a while. I left there after a couple years and moved to Austin, Texas. While there my car was repossessed so I had to whore around just to get a ride to work and for other reasons. Then I got tired of being there so I moved to California."

Robyn jumps as Reckless slides his hand between her legs. "What am I going to do with you?" she asks.

Reckless grins then takes another swig of Jack Daniels before continuing to finger Robyn. She ignores him. "I was engaged for a while. But my fiancé did not approve of my life style. I shouldn't have told him, but I was trying to be honest. He broke off the engagement, but by that time I was already pregnant. He went to prison a few months later, and I began sleeping around to pay the bills and to take care of my kids. He found out I had this guy named Ike sleeping over in the bed with me and his daughter, so he threatened to kill us both. I knew he was serious, he called big Rasheed, so I moved a couple times, had my mom change her phone number so he couldn't call and talk to the kids while they were in Arkansas for the summer, because his daughter would tell him where I lived. I have a son, Derrick, he's grown. His father hasn't been in touch since he was about five. I fucked up! I started sneaking out the window at night when I was thirteen years old. The guy I was sleeping with was twenty-eight."

Reckless snaps out of his stupor. "You were born to be a whore!" he yells then grabs her breast, pulling her back into the seat.

"I guess you can say that. I call it doing what a girl got to do," says Robyn.

"Well, come on over here and do me one more time, nice and slow," says Reckless as he unzips his pants then pushes her head down to his lap.

Skull looks over at Cynthia who's smiling. "What's your story?" he asks.

"I was born in Ohio. I married young after I got pregnant. But I was still sleeping around a lot and so was my husband. I just love to fuck what can I say. I've never really been happy with one man. My ex-husband was a lame. I basically married him for security. I'd gotten pregnant by him after losing the baby of the only man I truly loved. My mom and I argued over the pregnancy because the guy was a player and she threw a shoe and hit me in my stomach which caused a miscarriage. I lied and told the guy I'd gotten an abortion and from that day on things changed between us. I started snorting cocaine and the habit grew. When Robyn moved to Ohio from Arkansas, we became best friends. In fact, my ex-husband's brother became her man. For a while. But her husband found out and began kicking her ass and eventually left her, that's her son's father."

"What the hell did you expect?" Skull asks.

"I don't know, I guess we never really thought about it. Anyway, the father of her daughter, the one who went back to prison."

"Yeah," says Skull.

"He was like a brother to me. When he got into trouble he came to my home and got arrested. When he went to trial the prosecution called me as witnesses because they knew I used drugs and other stuff. All their witnesses said the guy who done the shooting had on black. And even though I knew that he didn't have on black that he had on a tan sweat suit, which he left on my bed. When I testified, I told the court and his attorney, I didn't see any tan sweat suit."

"What did the guy say?" Skull asks.

"Nothing, he just looked at me and told his attorney no more questions for me and I left."

"That's a hell of way to treat a brother. So I guess you're afraid for your life too, huh?" asks Skull.

"You could say that." Cynthia looks out the window and sees her girlfriend's home.

"Oh, that's the house, just pull up right there," she says before turning to look over the seat at Robyn.

"Are you done?" she asks. Reckless answers the question for her. "For now," he says, pulling up his pants.

Robyn smiles, takes her money from Reckless, then she and Cynthia get out the car closing the door.

"See you soon!" yells Cynthia.

"Sure," says Skull, before burning rubber, then roaring off down the road. Cynthia and Robyn begin walking up the steps to their friend Harriets home as she stands there on the porch, hands on hips, beaming at them. Harriet is short, about five-foot-five, light brown eyes, petite, cute, sassy, with an attitude to match! "It's about time you sluts made it here!" she yells. "What took you so long?" she asks. She then looks at the both of them and shakes her head. "Never mind." Robyn and Cynthia walk into her apartment arm in arm giggling.

Back at the station, Sissy, Detectives Brooks, and Taylor have arrived and are sitting in the captain's office. "So this is it?" the captain asks while looking at the drawing.

"Kevin says it is and he appears to have a very clear picture of what he seen in his mind," says Sissy.

"Okay, well, this is it then. Brooks, take this out to Charlotte and have her give it to the watch commanders so that they can make copies to pass among the patrol men on their shifts. In fact, have her call all shift commanders in for an emergency meeting."

"Yes, sir," says Brooks. He stands to leave, but suddenly has a question for the captain.

"Chief, has Lieutenant Jackson got back with you on the matter of getting black leaders out to help keep the peace?"

"Yes, he has, in fact we have a press conference shortly at one o'clock, where I plan to ask the public to help us find this car and its owner." The captain looks down at the small note on his desk.

"We have the Reverend Griffin and Pastor Witson from Mt. Sinai Baptist Church coming there, Imam Khalif from the Muslim community, and several high-ranking eldermen from across the city," he says.

"I sure hope it's enough," says Brooks before leaving out the door. Taylor turns to the captain. "Do you think broadcasting the description of the car publicly is a good idea? What if they dump the car?" he asks.

"Chances are that they may have already dumped it. But I doubt it," says the captain. "The owner of this car obviously put a lot of work into it. He's proud of this car and I believe he would have a hard time parting with it."

"I agree," says Sissy.

"Most men would rather divorce their wives, than abandon their cars. Not only that, but a car like this he'd want to show off to friends and on lookers. Maybe even race in the streets from time to time," Sissy suggests.

"Exactly," says Twyman. "Which is why I've decided to go public. Someone has seen this car and knows who the owner is and where he lives. I'd bet money that his ID is linked with that skull on the side with those red eyes."

As the captain is speaking his phone rings, he picks it up. "Yes! Okay, send her in." Everyone waits in silence as moments later a tall seasonally attractive woman knocks then enters into the office. Both Twyman and Taylor stand. Twyman coming from behind his desk.

"Ms. Laws, I'm a Captain Twyman. This is Detective Steve Taylor and Sissy Bonner our sketch artist."

They both greet her with hello. "This is Eloise Laws, one of the top criminal psychologist in the country," says Twyman. Eloise looks at Taylor, then Sissy.

"How do you do?" she says. Ms. Laws is tall, with reddish brown hair, a lovely smile, full lips and sparkling eyes. Her voice is very smooth and silky. She has the sound of a renowned jazz singer. Deep and raspy.

Twyman gestures to an empty chair. "Please, have a seat," he says before returning to his own chair.

"Eloise is going to help us build a profile on the suspects," says the captain.

"I'm going to do what I can," she says. "Typically we have found that the type of car these people drives expresses their approach to life. This person or person's lives in the fast lane. They probably have no permanent address, opting to sleep wherever they end up at the completion of their day. They probably have no long term relationships with women tending instead to frequent prostitutes or women they can pick up at a bar or club." Taylor looks up from his notes. "That would be a good place to begin a door to door search looking for this car," he suggests. Eloise agrees.

"Undoubtedly, it was a conversation piece out in the parking lot," she says.

"That's my belief also," says Sissy.

"Most importantly, you should know that the owner of this car has no problem killing." Eloise looks at everyone directly to stress this point. "He or they live for it. Maybe even worships it," she says.

Captain Twyman makes a note. "The skull with the red eyes symbolized a discard for life," says Eloise who is then interrupted by the phone ringing. The captain answers it. "Yes, fine, we are on the way." Twyman hangs up the phone then looks at his guest.

"It's time for the press conference. Let's not keep our public waiting," he says, smiling half-heartedly as everyone gathers their things to leave his office.

The captain then leads the way through the squad room out to the conference room where a host of reporters and black community leaders are already waiting. The captain walks in then steps up to the podium where he stands in front of a bank of microphones and motions for the crowd to quiet down. "May I have your attention please! You all are aware of the murders of the Davenport children a few days ago. We have a witness who has identified this vehicle and its occupants as the shooters. We want anyone who has seen this vehicle or knows anything about it or its owner, to contact us here at the station. We have set up a special line for this purpose. We are also offering a $50,000 dollar reward for anyone who can give us the shooter. Questions?"

A reporter in the back row raises his hand immediately. "Did this witness get a look at the shooter?" he asks.

"Yes," says the captain.

"Was it one shooter, two, what?" asks the reporter.

"There were two people in the vehicle, one climbed over the seat then over to the driver's side. We believe he done the actual shooting while the other guy drove."

A female reporter up front raises her hand.

"Yes." The Captain points to her. "If the witness saw two men in the car, what did they look like?" she asks.

Twyman looks over at Eloise and Taylor standing to the side, then back at the group in front of him. "They were white, with shaved heads," he says.

There is a rush of hands in the air as Twyman waives them down. "Listen, we are asking the people here in Mobile to remain calm and give us an opportunity to do our job and that they not take matters into their own hands." Another reporter raises his hand but asks his question without being recognized. "Captain Twyman, do you then believe that the murder of the Davenport children were racially motivated?"

"We don't know, beyond the obvious. But our criminal psychologist, Ms. Eloise Laws." He gestures toward her. "Has developed a criminal profile on the killers." The captain steps aside as Eloise steps up to the podium. "Good afternoon, though I am not prepared to say absolutely that the shootings were racially motivated, I am prepared to say that race was a factor. The person's responsible for these murders are very volatile and are capable in my opinion of outburst of violence unprovoked."

The same female reporter up front raises her hand again. "Why would they murder two children?" she asks.

"I can only speculate on that and right now it's not relevant. What is, however, is that anyone who knows these people should contact this station immediately. Simply knowing who these guys are could put them in harm's way."

Another reporter raises her hand. "Sabrina Harris with the Mobile Daily, are you suggesting these people would kill those who know their whereabouts or identity?"

"It's my belief that they would do anything to get away," says Eloise Laws.

Captain Twyman touches Eloise on the shoulder then whispers into her ear. Eloise nods her head yes, then steps aside. The captain then steps before the microphones. "That will be all the questions for now, the shift commander will be passing out a copy of the sketched vehicle and Ms. Laws profile of the shooters." Twyman steps away as the crowd and reporters group up asking questions among themselves regarding the shooters identity. *The Mobile Daily* reporter, Sabrina Harris is convinced that there is much more to this story than what's being told.

She turns to her sound/camera man Gerrome Williams. "Are you buying this crap, Gerrome?" she asks.

"Not at all," says Gerrome.

Sabrina is tall for a young woman and bowlegged. Her walk is incredibly sexy. She has gorgeous round dark eyes, a little sprinkle of freckles on her cheeks and nose. A smile that reveals a small gap between her two top front teeth. The fifth oldest of a number of sisters and brothers. Some by both her own parents and others after her parents divorced and built new separate lives. Sabrina is known for her tenacity among her journalist colleagues, she however, sums up her ability to find answers to the questions most people want to instinct, and growing up in a household with her sisters. Debra, Evon, Renay, and Alisha. "When you're raised in a home full of young boy-crazed girls, you develop an ear for the truth," she says. It was during this "boy crazed" period that she first met Gerrome. A small-built handsome guy, who happens to be the father of her niece by her sister Debra.

Gerrome removes the camera from his shoulder then turns it off. "We need to find out which detectives are on this case, and move when they move," he suggests. Sabrina nods her head in agreement as she watches Eloise Laws leave the room. "You're right, Mr. Williams, 'cause something in the milk ain't clean. Get everything packed up, I'll be right back. You know Sissy Bonner is my girl!" says Sabrina with a wink and a smile before disappearing into the squad room.

CHAPTER 6

Agents Branch and Oliver are sitting finishing lunch at their usual sports bar. The place is half empty, as they both watch the APB broadcast. Branch turns to Oliver. "I think we should pay the Captain another visit," he suggests. "I think we should begin using our own resources to find that car," says Oliver.

Branch agrees. "If that's all they have, then we already know all we need to know. I found that skull very interesting," says Branch.

"I believe it's his signature," says Oliver.

"What are the odds the Boss was watching?" Branch asks.

As Agent Branch is speaking his pager suddenly goes off, he stops and checks the number. "Guess who?" he asks. Oliver finishes off his drink then stands. "Duty calls," he says.

On the other end of town Robyn, Cynthia, and Harriet are sitting around laughing talking and drinking beer when Harriet sees the TV broadcast. "Ho, ho, hold up! They're talking about the killing of those two kids, turn it up!" she screams.

They all listen closely. Especially to Ms. Laws saying the killers may harm those who knew their identities. Robyn turns to Cynthia. "Oh, shit! Oh, shit!" she says then paces back and forth from the couch to the door. "Those motherfuckers are the killers! We were in that car! We slept with them for two days at Joe Earl's trailer."

Cynthia reaches up grabbing Robyn by the shoulder. "Calm down! Let's think this thing through," she says.

Robyn pulls away. "Fuck that, I'm outta here! Did you hear what that criminal bitch said? Did you hear?" she screams then walks back up to Cynthia. "She said that they would kill us to keep us silent. They know who we are!" she says.

"But why would they do that," asks Cynthia.

"We fucked them, they're not our men, we don't even know where they're from." Robyn walks back over by the TV.

"That don't matter, don't you see. We can identify them," she says. Harriet steps in between them. "Listen, that's all the more reason for you to call the police. Did you hear that part about the reward? Fifty thousand dollars! Now that's cheddar," says Harriet. Robyn walks over to the couch them throws herself down on it.

"Yeah, and we won't be able to spend a dime of it, if we are dead!" Cynthia sits down beside her.

"Hey, those guys are probably on their way out of state after discovering the police are looking for that car," she says.

"Fuck that shit!" says Harriet.

"What about that motherfucking reward, BITCHES! Fifty thousand dollars is a lot of money."

Robyn looks at Cynthia, then back to Harriet, "What would we have to do to get the money Harriet?" she asks.

"You'd have to ID them fuckers or give a description, since the police don't have any idea what them hoes look like," says Harriet.

Robyn stands up again and begins pacing. "I think we should just leave. I'm not looking for any trouble and I have my two boys to think about," she says.

"Well, what about those two children that were murdered like that, what about them?" Harriet asks. Neither Cynthia nor Robyn respond. "You two can't be the only people phoning in right now trying to get that fifty grand, including old Joe-Earl and the boys." Cynthia and Robyn glance at each other, then Robyn goes and sits down again. "It's up to you," she says.

"I would do it without the reward, but if I'm going to take a risk, I can use the money to move out of town," says Robyn.

Harriet walks over and takes the seat next to Cynthia. "Sure, the police are not going to tell them dick heads who ID them. You two didn't see the shooting, you're just saying you know what the crackers look like who drives that car with the big engine in front, and the skull with the red eyes on the back."

"What do you say?" Robyn asks, turning to Cynthia.

"Okay!" says Cynthia. "I'll call." Cynthia reaches for the phone. "Harriet, what was the number again?" she asks.

"Five, five, five, get your money, BITCH," says Harriet, laughing as she hands Cynthia the slip of paper with the number on it.

Malik is back at the house with Amin, Pup, Nino, and another ex-marine. Malik's old roommate monk who has recently arrived. Monk is short and stocky, with bulging arms and thighs. Like the rest of "Faze Two" he's a deep thinker. Amin is smoking mad after hearing what Detective Brooks told Malik earlier. "This shit don't surprise me at all!" he says.

"I didn't say anything but in the back of my mind, I knew Pup, I knew!" Pup turns to Malik. "The question is, how you want to handle this?" he asks.

Malik places his face in his hands, then rubs them back over his head. "Man, I'm tired of all this racist, fake white supremacy shit. I think it's time for it to end!" says Malik.

Nino slaps his thigh. "Well, let's end this shit, bro, once and for all, right now!" he says. Pup likes the idea too. "That's what I'm talking about, it's time these corn balls feel the black fist punched all the way through their face and their funny looking cone heads set on fire!"

Amin comes and stands in front of everyone. "Do ya'll know what we're talking about here. War! It ain't about fighting these chumps, it's about killing them. Everyone we find," he says. Monk joins the conversation. "Well, isn't that the very same type of killing they have done to us? I remember my grandmother telling me how in her day when whites would beat or lynch a black, or boil them in oil, or tie them to horses going in opposite directions to pull them apart, they would post a public announcement and on the day that the event were to take place, white women would put on their best outfit, dress the children up and prepare a basket of food, as if they were going on a picnic. The entire family found the death of black men, women and their children recreationally stimulating. And for some twisted reason beyond comprehension, they somehow think of us as the uncivilized, even today, we are the savages, the animals."

"I remember those stories, Monk!" says Malik. "One of the things I learned in the war is that if there is to be a war, it has to be final."

"There is no other way," adds Nino. "I read an autobiography of the great Zulu warrior and King, Shaka Zulu. He said: "never leave an enemy behind or they will rise again and seize your throat."

While everyone is reflecting on what Nino has just said, Amin shows no signs of calming down. "And that's exactly what has happened here in this country. This government is so stupid!" he says. "They allow these people to go around preaching hate and marching through the streets and they call it freedom of speech. Well, I for one believe that when you say things out of your mouth to promote hate and violence, to upset the normal flow of society, you then forfeit the right to speak freely!" Monk again breaks his silence. "All this serves a purpose in the overall plan man, controlled by this government, they're not total fools. They know what's up, hell, they've amended other parts of the Constitution and Bill of Rights when it suited their purpose. There was a time when the police couldn't come into your home without a search warrant. But they amended that, so now if the police think there is a crime going on, based on his good faith, it's cool."

Pup turns to Malik. "Again, my brother, I ask, where do we begin?"

"I want to compile as much information on these supremacy groups as I possibly can. Who trains them and their leaders around the country," says Malik. "I think we should find out who finances them also," Monk suggests.

Amin nods in agreement. "That's a good idea, they're just as guilty," he says.

Malik continues, "Once this is done, we can then decide on how to handle the operation."

Pup jumps up excitedly. "Hey, these people advertise their whereabouts in newspapers and magazines!"

"That's right!" says Monk.

"A person can just research and find out anything they want to know about these busters," says Nino.

Pup turns back to Malik. "Doesn't your brother-in-law run a firm that sets up advertising sites?" he asks.

"Yes, he does," says Malik.

"Then why not have him get the information that we need since he knows what he's doing and where to look," Pup inquires.

"I don't know, Hugh and I are not that close, and frankly, I don't really trust him all that well. His thing has always been to outshine me and I believe he has a hidden jealousy."

"Well, if he does, he should put that behind him. After all, it was his niece and nephew!" says Monk.

"Speaking of which," says Amin, "what do you have in mind for those two shooters if they are caught?"

"Well, they will have to be moved from the city jail to the county jail and my plan is to snatch them from the sheriff."

"I like that idea, but how are you going to do that?" Amin asks.

"We are going to box the car in at the light. You and I will come up from behind the car, secure the driver and the jailer, then get the keys. Terrible-T and the others will cover us unseen. Nino and Pup will then get the shooters and put them in the trunk of the front car. I've got a friend who owns a flower shop. We will leave the cars two blocks from the snatch, then all of you will get into this floral van and drive out here. I'll take my car and go home, because I know that is where the police will search first. Once the heat dies down, I'll come out here."

"What if they don't catch them?" Pup asks.

"They will be caught, I can feel it," says Malik.

Back at the station, Charlotte Lewis, the captain's secretary is on the phone talking to a caller. "May I ask the nature of the call Ma'am? Okay, well could you hold the line please?" says Charlotte as she looks around, asking if anyone has seen the captain. "A lady is on the phone stating that she can ID the driver of the car," she says.

Lieutenant Jackson is working nearby; he runs over. "Charlotte, I'll take the call!" he says. He then takes the receiver. "Ma'am, this is Lieutenant Brian Jackson speaking, can I help you?" he asks. "Yes, okay, no, no one has been paid the reward yet."

Onlookers around the station stand in silence listening to the lieutenant. "Okay, sure. Ma'am, I'm going to need both you and your girlfriend to come down to the station. Can you do that? Ma'am, where are you? I'll send a car to get you." Jackson writes the address down. "Okay, ma'am, I'll have a car there in five minutes." Hanging up he turns to the secretary. "Charlotte, get a car over to this address immediately and page Captain Twyman and tell him I need him here ASAP! We have two women who can ID the shooters."

"Yes, sir, should I send a plain car or patrolmen sir?" Charlotte asks.

"Make it plain, we want to get them here safely. Find Taylor and Brooks!" Jackson then turns, to see everyone seemingly frozen. "Let's move people!" he yells.

"Yes, sir!"

Immediately there's movement all around the station.

On the west side of town, Agents Branch and Oliver are sitting with their chief by the pool in his backyard. His wife Tammy walks out wearing a two-piece green linen short set. "Hello, boys, can I get you guys a cold glass of iced tea?" she asks.

"Yes, thank you," says Agent Branch.

"Me too," says Oliver.

Tammy looks at her husband. "I'm fine, honey," he says.

Tammy turns around and walks back into the house. Oliver turns back to the chief. "What's up, Boss?" Clarence smiles.

"I have no problem admitting that you guys were right, that you smelled this whole thing out from the beginning. You're both good agents," he says. Now the question is whether or not the Davenports were the beginning of a number of racial murders, like what took place in Atlanta?"

Branch crosses his legs. "I guess that would depend on whether or not we can ID the shooters and how quickly we can accomplish that," he says. Oliver smiles at the chief.

"But you already know that right, Boss?" asks Oliver.

Tammy returns before the chief can answer and places the tea in front of the agents. They thank her, she smiles approvingly.

"Enjoy!" she says before turning to walk back into the house. "Do you recall about four years ago, we were investigating a series of bank robberies in the Montgomery area?" asks the chief. Agent Branch nods his head.

"I do, Chief, we linked them to a white supremacy group. As I recall, there were a couple of murders involved in a couple of the hold-ups," he says.

"That's right, it was reported though never confirmed, that this man." Clarence slides a folder over to Agent Branch.

"Did the shooting for no reason, for the sheer enjoyment of it. His name is Michael Meyer, a.k.a. Reckless. The other guy is his longtime friend and fast car junkie, James Henson, a.k.a. Skull." Branch and Oliver high-five.

"Bingo!" says Branch excitedly. "Since these two are also wanted in connection with federal crimes, maybe Clayton and I should have another meeting with Captain Twyman."

"Yes, maybe since you two have something to offer this time he and his detectives will be a little more forthcoming?" says the chief.

Branch and Oliver finish up their drinks then stand to leave. "This is still off the record until we can place the car with Henson," the chief reminds his agents.

"We're on top of it, Boss," says Oliver with a salute and a mischievous grin.

The agents walk out the side gate to their car, get in, then pull off. Agent Branch is driving this time, he turns to Oliver. "I understand the bank robbery, these supremacy groups recruit nobodies and make them feel like they have value by giving them the survival of the white race as their cause, and they use the stolen money as support. But the killing of those children appear to be nothing more than an act of ignorant violence," he says.

83

"I can't figure that one out either." Oliver scratches his head. "The thing about this survival of the white race agenda is that no one is attacking, nor randomly killing whites. Every other nation of people are very content with who they are and are living their lives. But these people are obsessed with murdering people who have never gone after them. I'll never understand it," says Oliver. The agents continue the rest of their drive in silence.

It's early evening. Cynthia and Robyn have just arrived at the station and are being ushered toward the captain's office. Taylor and Brooks are seated inside. The captain walks over to open the door. "Ms. Davis and Ms. Ware, come in and have a seat." He then turns to the crowd outside his office. "Clear out!" he yells. Closing the door, then turning back to the hookers. "Sorry about that," he says as he moves back around his desk retaking his seat.

"Now you two ladies say that you know the driver of the car we posted?"

Robyn speaks up. "Well, we don't really know them. We kinda just slept with them last night," she says.

"Yeah," says Cynthia. We don't know their real names or anything or where they live. They were over a neighbor's trailer the other day when we went over," Cynthia adds pointedly.

"Ms. Davis, Ms. Ware, I'm Detective Brooks and this is Detective Taylor."

Cynthia and Robyn nod their recognition.

"Can you tell us where this trailer park is located, and its name?"

Robyn leans forward. "It's the John's Park Trailer Home. North of here. My neighbor's name is Joel-Earl," she says.

"How long have you known Mr. Earl?" Brooks asks.

"About four years. He's a good old boy, even claims to be racist, but like most of them including some of our past presidents he's fascinated with black women sexually and his money is green," says Robyn with an ironic dignity.

Brooks ignores the last statement. "Have you ever seen the two men that you were with there before?" he asks.

"No, not until a couple of days ago," says Robyn.

Taylor looks up from playing with a piece of lent on his slacks. "What did you call them?" he asks.

Cynthia answers the question. "The one I was with was called Skull, because people used to say that the things he would do was crazy, like out of his skull. The one Robyn was with called himself Reckless."

"When do we get the reward?" Robyn demands.

Twyman smiles and claps his hands together. "Ms. Ware, first of all, you two have to talk with our sketch artist and give her a description of these men. The reward is for providing information that captures them. You two have already said that you do not know where they live, their real names or where they have gone."

Robyn jumps to her feet, grabbing her handbag. "I told you we should not have gotten involved in this. I knew they would pull this kinda shit!" she screams.

Twyman lowers his voice then rises from his seat. "Now hold on, I haven't said that you have not been a big help, or that you will not be given a reward for what information you've provided. I'm saying we need you to give us a description. We will talk with Joel-Earl, and then determine just how much your information has been worth in dollars."

Robyn turns to look down at Cynthia. "Our ultimate aim is to capture these two and we need to keep some kind of incentive out there for someone to provide the information we need in finding them. You understand?" Cynthia and Robyn look at each other.

The captain continues, "Now I need you two to go with our sketch artist." He turns and presses a button on his phone. "Charlotte, tell Sissy to come in here," he says.

A moment later Sissy walks in. "Yes, Captain?" she asks.

"This is Ms. Davis and Ms. Ware. They are going to provide you with a description of our two suspects." Sissy opens the door all the way and smiles. "If you two would come with me, please," she says. They both stand then follow Sissy out into the station.

Twyman closes the door behind them then turns back to Brooks and Taylor. "I want you two to go have a talk with Mr. Joel-Earl," he says. As the detectives are gathering themselves to leave, Agent branch and Oliver knock on the captain's door before walking into his office. Agent Oliver is first.

"Good evening, Captain," he says.

Twyman acknowledges them. "Agent Branch and Oliver, pull up a chair," says the captain.

"Thank you," they say in unison.

The captain turns to his detectives. "These are the two agents I told you about earlier. Agents, these are my Detectives Steve Taylor and Tracy Brooks." They all shake hands. "Now, gentlemen, what can I do for you?" the captain asks.

"We may be able to do something for you, Captain," says Branch as he hands Captain Twyman the folder with the photos and information on Skull and Reckless.

"Who are these two?" Twyman asks.

"That one there is Michael Meyer, a.k.a. Reckless. The other one is James Henson, a.k.a. Skull. We believe they are the shooters in the Davenport case, as well as in a string of Federal Bank robberies," says Agent Branch.

Taylor reaches for the photo. "May I take a look at those, Chief?" he asks.

Twyman passes him the photos then takes his seat. Inwardly, he's realizing everything else the agents said previously, may also come true. "Those two, Detective Taylor are known to be a part of a white supremacy group known for unprovoked murder and violence. We still believe that the Davenports could be the start of a rash of murders, similar to those in Atlanta," says Oliver. "But the guy who done those murders was apprehended and is now in prison," says Taylor.

"And he was black." Brooks adds.

Branch glances at Oliver then at the detectives. "Wayne Williams was a fall guy," he says. "He was set up by higher-ups in the federal government because they feared a race riot. They didn't want to see little white boys and girls murdered randomly in retribution for what had been done to black children. Wayne fit the bill perfectly. He was a loner and considered somewhat strange by those in his community," says Branch.

"That makes sense," Taylor agrees.

"So with a black man convicted of the murders, there was no one to lash out at?" says Brooks.

"Exactly," says Branch. "But not only that, what most people don't realize is that Wayne was only convicted of two of the murders, on very flimsy evidence, coached testimony, and scientific reports which had either been altered or were outright lies."

Captain Twyman weighs into the discussion. "So what actually are we up against here?" he asks.

"A group of radicals or two renegades looking to start something?"

"We won't know that until we capture them," Oliver suggests.

"Hold on a minute," says the captain as he presses the button again on his phone. "Charlotte, would you have Sissy bring Ms. Davis and Ms. Ware back to my office, please." The captain releases the button turning back to the agents. "We have two women here with our sketch artist who said they met these two a couple days ago at their friend's trailer."

"Yeah." Brooks grins. "They came here hoping they would get the reward we offered. They even slept with these guys."

Agent Branch smiles. "That must have been a thrill," he says.

Cynthia and Robyn walk in. The agents try to hide their shock that the whores are black. Captain Twyman sits on the edge of his desk. "Special Agents Branch and Oliver, this is Cynthia Davis and Robyn Ware." They exchange greetings. Sissy steps inside closing the door. "The agents have provided us with a couple photos I'd like you to look at," says the captain. He takes the two photos out of the folder and hands one to each of the hookers. They both instantly recognize Reckless and Skull. "Are these the two men you met at the trailer park?" the captain asks.

They both nod their heads. "Yes, that's them," says Robyn.

"How did you know it was them?" asks Cynthia.

"Does that mean we won't get any money?" asks Robyn. The captain gets Sissy's attention. "Sissy, have someone take the ladies home. Ladies, thank you for your time and effort," he says.

"This way, ladies," says Sissy but as she opens the door, Robyn looks at her then tosses the photo across the room. "Oh! You got those pictures, so you don't need us anymore, is that it? We risked our lives to come tell you all this shit and all we get is a motherfucking ride back home!" she screams, enraged.

"I told Cynthia this was all bullshit, that y'all don't give a fuck about us!" yells Robyn.

Agent Branch stands up. "That's not true, ladies. Actually, it's you who don't give a damn about yourselves. Coming here was no risk to your lives, in fact you may be saving them."

Both Robyn and Cynthia glare at the agent as he continues. "The only risk to your lives was when you slept with men you didn't even know just to make a dollar! They could have killed you too. You're black."

"You don't know shit about us!" shouts Cynthia.

"You're right," says Agent Branch. "But I know there are millions of women out there struggling every day to pay bills, to take care of their children and other needs. They go to school, they study at home, work two jobs, sometimes three, but they never disrespect themselves for a few dollars. No material possession in the world is worth that."

Robyn rolls her eyes then hikes up her skirt placing her hand inside her panties. "PUSSY POWER," she says before turning to Cynthia. "Let's get the fuck out of here before I catch a case." She then pulls Cynthia out the door.

Twyman turns back to Oliver. "I'm going to call a press conference and get these photos out on the air so that we can get these two," he says. "We have a few things we need to do," Agent Oliver says. "In the meantime, if anything develops, we'd expect a call."

"You can count on it," says the captain, extending his hand to Branch then Oliver in a firm handshake. He then punches the button on his intercom. "Charlotte, set up a news conference, we have photos of the shooters!"

"Right away, sir!" Charlotte then turns to the crowd around her desk. "We've got them!" The station erupts in cheers and applause.

It's late evening, not quite sunset. Malik and Hugh Lamont are walking down a path in a densely wooded area, just south of the city. The path leads to a clearing where Malik and some of the other guys would come to hang out, smoke weed, or spend time with their ladies years ago. "I haven't been out here in a long time. Hugh, you sure we are on the right path?" Malik asks.

"Yeah, it's right up here," says Hugh. Thirty yards more and they walk into the clearing.

"It still looks the same," says Malik as he looks around reminiscing.

"Why wouldn't it?" says Hugh.

"Shit dies and grows back every year. But that's not why you brought me out here, so what's up?" he asks. Malik walks over to him. "I need your expertise."

"You could have asked me that over the phone. What? You want to start an ad looking for info on the killers?" Hugh asks.

"I already have all the info I need, I know who killed my son and daughter. And I believe I know why, I'm just waiting for their capture," says Malik.

"So you want something to aid in their capture?" Hugh asks.

"No, I want all the information you can get from the databases that belong to white supremacy groups!"

"Why?"

"Because they murdered my babies!"

"How do you know that?" asks Hugh.

"Because Kevin saw them do it," says Malik.

"What!" Hugh is surprised.

"Yeah, he was so shook up that he ran and hid in his closet."

"Damn! I can't believe it!"

Malik follows him. "Believe it 'cause that's what it is man, and it's been that way for way too long. Everyone is walking around in shock, but that's over for me, I seen too much death in the core, I'm immune to it," says Malik.

"So why do you want info from their databases?" asks Hugh Lamont.

"Because it's time for them to bleed, it's time for them to know what it's like to be hunted, set on fire, tortured, cut into pieces, lynched."

"Malik, you're crazy!" Hugh turns away from him.

"I'm the reality of my experiences," says Malik.

"You're asking for big trouble!" Hugh warns.

"I'm not asking for nothing but the names, locations, and rank of the supremacy groups and if possible, their financial backers. Let's start with those here in Alabama," says Malik. "You've not thinking clearly, you should go home and talk with Sakinah and Ms. Norma."

Malik ignores him. "Do you know that this entire society that we live in is a white supremacy group? Well, it is. Sure there are whites who are as against racism as you and I, and they have fought in the streets, and died doing so beside our people. Latinos, Native Americans, and Asians. But the harsher reality is that our governing bodies, those with the money and the power those involved in its hidden societies, laboratories and think tanks have always allowed these people to co-exist in our world. To preach hate, murder, to incite violence—all this while the big hat boys sit back and pull the stings. All of us down here on the bottom, including the racist, are nothing more than puppets, pawns. They keep our lives in turmoil, and covertly assist and finance it from their yachts anchored in some foreign waters, or while they're fucking their secretaries during lunch time on Capitol Hill, or the White House."

Hugh stands up then walks over by a large boulder near the cliff, Malik follows him there also. "That is until the hate backfires. Do you recall the two white high school students in Littleton, Colorado who walked into their high school, then shot and killed only the students who they believed were superior to them, including one black?"

"Yes, I remember," says Hugh.

"Fourteen others were hospitalized, a few were in critical condition, and the two killed themselves," he says.

"That's correct," says Malik. "Now when this happened, twenty-four hour news coverage was given to this event. So called experts came out the woodwork trying to explain it from a psychological perspective on all the morning and nightly talk shows. US Congressmen and Senators proposed new legislation. The President drafted a new gun control law overnight. Everyone wanted to know how? Why?

But none of these people stepped up to answer the big question, from the President on down. No one proposed legislation dealing with removing white supremacy and racial material from the public view. No one! Guns don't kill people, people who point them and pull the trigger do! Thousands of Blacks and Latin American inner city youths die across the country every week. No Presidential Proposal? No Congressional Legislation. White children across the country are being preyed upon by this racist system which trains and teaches them to falsely believe they are superior to blacks, Asians and every other non-white. But when they look around, they see that's not true. And as a result of this brain washing they lose their own self-worth, which makes them suicidal and prone to violence against others. Those who make it beyond high school, are the ones responsible for driving up and shooting blacks and browns or standing on the steps of their city building, recruiting and promoting more people to follow in that path. All with the governing bodies covert permission."

"What does all that have to do with you and what you've asked me to do?" Hugh demands.

"I'm getting to that!"

"Is this going to be a long story?" Hugh asks, clearly aggravated.

Malik stares at him then continues, "In the secret society known as the Tri-Lateral Commission, their main theme is to use opposites to bring about change. Unknowingly to most poor black folk, this opposite, racism, was used to give this governing body more power in the lives of its citizens through civil rights legislation. Black folks seen it as good, yeah, we can vote now! The thing is, they could always vote, and do all the other things guaranteed by the Constitution, they just weren't man enough to take what was theirs! The Klans nightriders and other greedy hillbillies in government punked us, taught us fear and to doubt ourselves, our own strength," says Malik.

"I'm not going to be a part of any killings, period!" Hugh protests.

"I just want you to know that it's time to rid the world of the opposite, and once it's gone, this government, and the cowardly white supremacist hiding in their judges' chambers, the White House, the Senate and their Congressional Chambers, the ones at the Pentagon, and CIA headquarters dreaming up these biological agents that attack only people with the melanin molecule will know that the game is over. Their reign has brought nothing but destruction, to the land, the ocean, the air and to people all over the globe."

Hugh Lamont gets up off the rock then heads back toward the path to leave. "I'll have to think about this and get back with you," he says.

"You do that," says Malik as he sits back on the boulder, watching Hugh leave, shaking his head.

"Big mistake," says Malik to himself.

CHAPTER 7

It's the next morning. Patricia is in her office at the law firm. The walls of her office are lined with framed photos of her mother, father, and the grandparents who started the firm, along with their parents. At the front of the building, her daughter Jada is entering the lobby. She passes by the secretary. "Hello, Janice! Is my mom in her office?" she asks.

Janice looks up from what she's doing. "Oh, hi, Jada, yes, she is, go right in," she says.

Jada passes through the lobby, which is decorated paying tribute to black jazz legends. The likes of Billy Holiday, Sara Vaughn, Eartha Kitt, Miles Davis, Charlie Parker, Monk, Ella Fitzgerald, just to name a few. She knocks then enters her mom's office.

Pat sits back in her chair. "Hi, honey, what brings you here?" she asks.

Jada kisses her mom then sits down at her desk. "Mom, I'm worried about Malik, and so is Sakinah. I think she hasn't really said anything, I just feel it."

"I don't think there is anything to worry about," says Patricia. "I think he's handling this very well."

"Mom, you know Malik and I were practically raised together. I know him, and I know he has something on his mind other than the death of Kazi and Eunique," Jada insists.

"Honey, your cousin is a very strong man, very intelligent, and more than able to take care of himself. Now I think I know him well enough to say that if he were in any kind of trouble or anything, he would come to me and let me know about it. I think you are worrying about nothing," says Patricia.

"Mom," says Jada clearly frustrated. She stands then comes around the desk. "I had a dream last night. I don't know what's going on, I just know something is about to happen, and I'm scared Mom!" Patricia gets up and embraces her daughter. "It's okay, baby, Malik is fine, and he's going to stay that way," she says.

She kisses Jada on the forehead then holds her tightly looking off in thought, knowing Jada has put in words what she was afraid to say.

It's late evening. Malik is at home with Sakinah sitting at the breakfast nook. "Aunt Pat called for you earlier, Malik, she wants you to be sure to call her."

"I will, I'm thinking about taking a couple of months off from the firm. I need some time off," says Malik.

"I think that's a really good idea, you want to go to Baltimore?" Sakinah asks.

"No, I don't want to go anywhere. I have a project I want to spend some time on," he says.

"Was that what you and Hugh Lamont were working on?" asks Sakinah.

"No, we just spoke about some data, I think I'll be needing in the near future."

The phone rings, Sakinah picks it up; it's Ms. Norma. "Hello," she says.

"No, Malik, turn on the television!" Malik reaches and turns the TV set on that sits on the countertop. Captain Twyman is at a live news conference showing the photos of the two men wanted in the killing of the children. Malik and Sakinah listen in silence.

"Here, Malik." Sakinah hands him the phone, retaking her seat. She's crying again. "Yes Mother, I know, she's okay, I will, always Mom. I love you too. I'll call you later Inshaallah." Malik hangs up the phone, turns off the television, then walks over to Sakinah and rubs her shoulders. He then kisses her on the cheek. "Stay strong, sweetheart, it's almost over. I promise you that."

Reckless and Skull are at a redneck bar on the outskirts of town. They are not aware of the news broadcast, but the bartender and owner, a heavyset, hairy-chest guy, with twitching eyes is watching. He recognizes the two instantly. He calls the waitress over who has just come to the bar for more beer for the two. She's brunette with dark brown eyes, a strong figure. "Tracy James, are those two guys still back there shooting pool? Tracy James glances over at the news broadcast on the small TV behind the bar."

"Oh my God!" She grabs at her mouth, instantly realizing how loud she's spoken. "Those are the two guys who shot those kids!" she says.

"Shh, keep it quiet, there is a reward for those two. If we can keep them here until the police gets here, we can collect it," says the bar owner with a greedy, devilish smile.

Tracy turns and looks around the bar. Except for Reckless and Skull in the back, there are only five others in the bar. Two couples and one guy who looks more asleep than awake. The bar is a small hole in the wall with two large rooms and toilets. The main room has the bar area, the other room has four pool tables, an old jukebox and his and her toilets.

"Ah, Fred, I don't know," Tracy James says. "Those guys are murderers, I'm afraid," she says.

"Listen," Fred says soothingly. "There is nothing to be afraid of. I'm calling the police. You take them their drinks and talk friendly to them. For that, I'll give you ten thousand dollars of the reward."

"For that you'll give me half!" yells Tracy.

"Fifteen," says Fred.

Tracy doesn't move. "Seventeen and I'll let you keep your job."

Tracy smiles. "Okay," she says. Tracy picks up the tray with the drinks then heads toward the pool room. Fred calls to her. "Open a couple of buttons on that top," he says. Tracy looks back at him, frown but does as he asks before entering the pool table area where Skull and Reckless are playing. Fred doesn't hesitate; he picks up the phone then dials the police. "My name is Fred Allen. I'm the owner of the Blue Room Bar out on Sixth Street. The two guys you're looking for that killed those kids are here in the back of my place shooting pool. Yeah, yeah, I'm sure. Yeah, make sure you bring the reward with you, and enough money to cover any damages to my place. Hello? Hello!" Fred hangs up the phone. "Damn cops!" mumbles Fred.

Tracy James arrives back in the pool room with the drinks. She's trying as best she can not to appear nervous, hoping Fred has called the police and that they will hurry up and get there. If only she didn't need the money. She takes a deep breath before entering the pool table area. "Here you are gentlemen, will there be anything else?" She asks.

"Yeah," Skull slurs.

"How about you crawling up on this here pool table and pulling that little skirt?"

Reckless interrupts him by punching Skull in the arm. "Naw! Naw! Not while I'm kicking your ass and the loser has to pay for drinks," he says.

"Hell, I'll pay for the drinks, and a few dollars more to drink her bath water." Skull grabs Tracy, pulling her to him; she gives him a nervous smile.

"Please don't," she says.

"Ah, come on let's finish this last game, you dumb shit!"

Reckless snatches Skull by his vest and yanks him off Tracy.

"Okay, okay, here, honey." Skull takes some change out of his pocket. "Go put on some real foot stompin' music, 'cause once I'm done whipping his ass, you and me gonna dance the night away," he says.

Tracy takes the money then goes to the jukebox to make a selection. Skull walks back over to Reckless. "Come on shit for brains." He slaps Reckless on the head.

"Let me finish kicking your ass!" Skull then sets up for his shot, as Reckless steps to the side. "Hey, you think we ought to stop back over there by those hookers place tonight?" Reckless asks.

"I got that on my mind." Skull points at Tracy James over by the jukebox. "But oh, what's her name sure did make me feel right nice," says Skull.

"You should have seen what oh Robyn was doing to me in the back seat. Ooh wee!" screams Reckless.

"She's better out the bed then she is in. I should have made her pay me the twenty dollars instead of me giving it to her," he says. They both laughed then take a swallow of their beers.

Tracy James finishes making her selections then walks back over to the table. "You boys from around here?" she asks.

"Yeah." Skull burps.

"What parts?" she asks.

"Why you wanna know?" Reckless asks.

"I'm just asking, that's all," she says.

"Don't mind him, little darling," says Skull, placing his arm around her.

"I'll tell you everything you need to know after this game is over. Now you just sit your pretty little self down right here and keep those pretty little brown eyes on ole Skull, okay?"

"All right," Tracy James says nervously, closing one of the buttons she had opened earlier. Outside the bar, Captain Twyman has just pulled into the parking lot with a number of other police cars. The sun is setting, but everyone notes the car Kevin described parked out in front of the bar, even the Skull with the red eyes.

Detectives Taylor and Brooks pull up alongside Agents Branch and Oliver. They all exit their cars then walk over toward Captain Twyman, adjusting their gun holsters and vests. Branch looks at the suspect's vehicle again then back at the Captain.

"Looks like they are here," he says.

"The owner of the place saw the broadcast and called. He's sure it's them," says the captain.

"How you want to handle this?" Branch asks.

"According to the owner, they're still in the back playing pool and did not see the broadcast. I'm going to send a couple undercover officers in with hidden radio and camera to spot them then give us a location."

The captain signals for the two plain clothes officers, one male and the other female, to move inside. "Now, I don't doubt that they are armed, but we want to avoid a shootout. I don't want innocent people killed," he says.

The captain then walks over to the police car with the others that has the monitor connected to the mini camera that the spotter officers are wearing. They all see inside the place. The captain gets Agents Branch and Oliver's attention. "You two can go in with Detectives Taylor and Brooks, they're already wired. Some of you go around the back and cover the door. Stay out of sight!"

Several officers head toward the back of the Bar making sure to take cover. Taylor, Brooks, Oliver, and Branch enter the bar first. Taylor walks up to the bar tender. "Are you Freddie Allen, sir?" Fred puts the bar towel down.

"Yes, I am."

"Then you called about the suspects?" asks Taylor.

"Yea, yea, they're still in the back playing pool," says Fred.

Taylor looks around the bar area.

"Listen, I want you to quietly go over to your customers one by one and ask them to get up and step out front quickly and quietly." Fred tosses his hands up then comes from behind the bar. Agents Branch and Oliver move toward the back as the two couples pass on their way out. They peep inside the pool room to see Reckless and Skull still engaged in their game. Branch smiles. Tracy is still sitting in the chair, but Branch manages to get her attention then motions for her to come out. She lets him know that she understands.

"Hey, would you guys like another beer?" she asks.

Again Tracy James manages a smile. "Sure, baby," Skull says.

"And bring some of those wing things," yells Reckless.

"Okay, I'll be right back." Tracy stands up, fighting the impulse to run she manages to walk out as Skull turns back to his game.

Agent Branch stops Tracy as she enters the main part of the bar and tells her to go outside. He then calls Brooks, Taylor, and Oliver over. They all take out their weapons. "On three," he says.

"One, two, three!" They all rush into the pool room screaming. "Freeze!"

"Don't move!"

"Put your hands up!" Reckless reaches for his gun, but Branch points his directly at his head. "Put your hand on it and you'll be dead before it clears your vest!" he says. Reckless puts his hands on the pool table, swearing as he does so. Skull makes a move to go around the table, but Brooks walks up on him with his gun aimed at his chest.

"That bitch! She set us up! She called the cops!" shouts Skull.

"Shut your mouth!" orders Taylor. "Each one of you put your hands behind your head and clasp your fingers."

While Branch and Oliver cover them, Taylor and Brooks move in close to pat them down. Taylor takes the gun from Reckless, then they cuff then both. Taylor calls Twyman to let him know it's all clear.

Oliver steps up to the suspects. "You two are under arrest for not only the Davenport murders, but for federals bank robberies and murder. You have the right to remain silent." He reads them their rights.

"I don't know nothing about no murders or robberies!" yells Skull. "This is bull shit man, you got the wrong guys. We were just having a beer and a game of pool man!" yells Reckless as Twyman walks in. "Have ballistics get busy on that firearm and get these two out of here, before we have a media circus outside!" he says.

Taylor and Brooks hand the suspects over to two patrolman. Taylor stops beside Branch. "I'm sure glad this is over," he says.

"Don't be so sure," says Branch.

"What do you mean by that?" Taylor asks.

"All we have is a little kid who said he seen a racing car with a skull on it. He didn't ID the people in the car."

"Well, the car he ID is parked out front and it fits the description he gave us," says Taylor. Twyman interrupts them.

"We can iron all this out at the station. Let's go." They all turn and head back into the bar area where Fred Allen is waiting for them. He walks up to the captain.

"Listen, when do I get my reward? You got these guys, I called it in," says Fred.

"You'll get your reward. I'll send someone to talk with you in a couple of days."

The officers all head out the door. Fred screams after them, "yeah don't forget. If I don't hear from you, I'll come see you! Damn cops!" Fred turns back to cleaning the shot glasses left on the top of the bar.

Outside, Reckless and Skull are sitting in the back of two separate police cars. One reporter has made it to the scene and as Twyman comes out the door of the Bar, she rushes up to him. "Captain Twyman, I'm Sabrina Harris. I'm with the Mobile Daily. Can you tell me what lead to the arrest of the suspects?"

"No, I cannot, not at this moment."

Twyman continues walking toward his car and so does everyone else. Sabrina follows him. "Well, can you tell me whether or not this will be a death penalty case?" she asks.

"That's up to the district attorney," says the captain as he opens the door to his car, gets in, closes it, then lets down the window. "Can you tell me why the FBI is involved in this case?" Sabrina persists.

"Ms. Harris, all the answers to your questions will be forth coming after we complete our investigation. Until then, there is really nothing I can say. Now if you would excuse me." The captain turns to his driver. "Let's go!" The caravan of police head out of the parking lot with their lights flashing.

Malik, Sakinah, Lenora, and Kevin are sitting in the Davenport's living room. Kevin is standing between Malik's legs.

"Kevin, you want to go with me tomorrow to see your uncles Amin and Pup? They've been asking about you."

Kevin turns to Lenora. "Mom, can I?"

"It's okay with me, that's if Malik wants to be bothered with you all day," she says.

"It's no bother at all, in fact, the city fair starts this weekend. We may as well drop on by and see what we can win," says Malik as he lifts Kevin slightly off his feet.

Kevin is really excited about the fair. "Can we get some cotton candy and some caramel apples?" he asks.

"Sure, but I don't think your mom wants you eating a lot of candy?" says Malik.

"I'll brush my teeth really good afterward!" says Kevin, giving his mom his pleading look.

Malik smiles, tickles Kevin, then picks him up and gives him a kiss. "Let's you and me go out by the pool and have a man to man," he says. Kevin laughs and waves good bye to his mom as Malik carries him out the room toward the patio door.

Sakinah watches them smiling at their relationship. "You know Malik loves Kevin," she says.

"The feeling is mutual," says Lenora, smiling also at the two of them. "Kevin never said anything, but I believe he thought Malik would be mad at him because he seen what happened."

"We talked about that. Malik was worried that Kevin seeing what happened would somehow affect him," says Sakinah. "It has, he's been sleeping with me ever since. I try to spend as much time with him as I can and I've explained to him what racism is and why these people do what they do the best I can, but he keeps asking," says Lenora.

"I know that's a challenge," Sakinah says.

"It really is. After I'm done, his last question is always: "But, Mom, why would they do that to a kid? We didn't do nothing to them." Lenora and Sakinah just sit and look at each other with no answer for the madness that suddenly invaded their lives.

Outside Malik and Kevin are sitting by the pool. Malik has Kevin on his lap. "You know, Kevin, I'm really proud of you," he says.

"For what?" Kevin asks.

"Because you're a good guy."

"I am?" asks Kevin.

"Yes, you are. It takes a lot of courage not to be afraid to stand up and tell the truth. A lot of adults are afraid to stand up for what's right," says Malik.

"They are?" asks Kevin.

"Of course," says Malik.

"But why?" asks Kevin.

"Because they know nothing about Heaven. Most of them don't believe in it. They say they do, but they don't really. They know only this physical life. They are afraid to do anything that will cause them to leave it."

"Where is heaven?" asks Kevin.

"Heaven is mental. It's a state of mind. Can you see your thoughts?" Malik asks.

"I don't think so. I just think things," says Kevin.

"That's right. When you do good things, you feel good and happy. But before you actually do it, you think it. When you help people that are worse off than you, the hungry, the poor, the sick and they feel better, that's heaven," says Malik.

"I had a jar full of bumblebees once," says Kevin. "And they kept flying around in the jar, trying to get out. I knew they were not happy, so I let them go and they flew away!"

"Did letting them go make you happy?" asks Malik.

"Yes," says Kevin.

"Well, that's heaven. Listen, inside your body, you have what's called a soul. It's locked inside just like you had those bee's locked in the jar. Allah put the soul in the body and when he wants to set it free, he opens the body and lets the soul go free."

Kevin looks at Malik puzzled. "How does he do that?" he asks.

"This is what we call death or dying. It's what happened to Kazi and Eunique," says Malik. "But they were shot with a gun?" Kevin places his head on Malik's chest.

"That's true, but Allah uses all kinds of ways to open up the body so the soul can fly free. Some of these look really bad. But the soul doesn't feel any pain or hurt."

"Even if it's hit by a train?" asks Kevin.

"It doesn't matter. As long as the soul has been good while it was in the body and it had courage to do what was right. No matter how the body was opened up the soul will never feel any pain."

"Are Kazi and Eunique in Heaven?" Kevin asks.

"Yes, children go to heaven automatically. They are together now, playing, laughing, having fun," says Malik.

"Who are they playing with?" Kevin asks. "Each other, other children whose souls were set free while they were young and the angels."

"Wow! Will I be able to play with the angels when my soul is free?"

"Yes, you will," says Malik.

Kevin jumps down excited. "I'm going to tell mom, Kazi and Eunique are playing with real angels. I'm going to play with them too!" he yells.

"Hold on," says Malik. "Come here for a minute."

Kevin walks back up to Malik. "I love you and I'm here for you anytime you want to do something, play on just hang out."

"Okay, I love you too, Malik," says Kevin.

"Give me a big hug."

Kevin does then runs back into the house screaming about playing with the angels. Malik sits back in his chair looking up at the stars. Wondering how much longer he will be able to protect Kevin.

Back at the city building, Reckless and Skull have arrived. They are being held in separate holding rooms. Twyman, Taylor, Brooks, Oliver, and Branch are standing outside their doors planning their interrogation method.

"I think you four should pair up, state and federal, so these clowns know they are cornered on both levels," Twyman suggests.

Taylor turns to Branch and Oliver. "That works for me, whichever one of you wants to team with me on the shooter, let's get with it," he says.

Branch steps up. "My pleasure."

Oliver steps over to Brooks. "I guess the driver belongs to you and me," he says.

"After you," Brooks gestures.

They both enter the interrogation room. Skull is sitting in a chair still hand cuffed from behind. He has a wild look in his eyes. Oliver and Brooks walk over to him. "Michael Meyer, I'm FBI Special Agent Clayton Oliver. And this is Detective Brooks. You've already been read you rights, is there anything you want to tell us that we could use in keeping you out of the electric chair for the murder of the two Davenport children?"

"I don't know nothing about no murder of no kids, man," Skull screams. "I ain't got nothing to say to you!"

"You should know that we have an eyewitness who ID your car. That's how we found you," says Brooks. "They also saw your partner climb into the back seat, while you drove up on those two children and he shot them from point-blank range. If you want to die for him, it's okay with us," says Oliver.

Skull is visibly shaken. "Uh, can...can I have a cigarette, man?"

Brooks glances over at Oliver. "Sure, Agent Oliver would you give Mr. Meyer a cigarette please?"

Oliver smiles then walks over to Skull. "Okay, as long as he realizes that ninety days from now, his ass may be smoking?" The officers both grin at Skull.

Across the hall, Agents Branch and Taylor are in the room with Reckless. He's cuffed and shackled to the floor.

"Fuck you and fuck this shit, man, I don't know nothing about no kids getting shot man. I ain't got shit to tell you, fuckers!" screams Reckless as he tries to break free!

Taylor places his chair next to Reckless. "You may not have to Mr. Reckless, can I call you Reckless?" Taylor asks with a smile. "You see when ballistics comes back on your gun, the entire story will have been told."

"Yeah," says Branch. "And when it's told, I see you in the electric chair, wishing you had never gotten that first toy gun for Christmas," laughs Agent Branch.

"Fuck you!" screams Reckless, jerking on his chairs.

"No, fuck you and your white supremacy bullshit!" Branch yells back.

Across the hall Oliver and Brooks are still working on Skull. Brooks grabs his attention. "Tell me something, Skull. Why in the world would you guys murder two little children? I can't understand that. Look at these." Brooks opens the folder on the table, containing the photos of Kazi and Eunique. "This is Kazi and Eunique. Beautiful, aren't they? Now, this is the photos of them after you shot them in their heads."

Skull turns his face away. "I didn't kill those kids!" he yells.

"Yes, you did!" says Brooks.

Oliver steps in front of him. "You drove the car!" he says.

"But I didn't shoot them!" Skull says.

"Who did?" Brooks asks.

"I…I…don't want to talk no more, I need to think," yells Skull.

"Think!" screams Brooks, before jumping to his feet.

"You're not a thinker, if you were, you wouldn't be sitting here trying to protect Henson. You want to know why," Brooks asks.

"Sure," says Skull.

"Because we have his gun and once we match it with the bullets taken from the children, it's all over. We already have your car at the scene." Skull drops his head down on the table, shaking uncontrollably.

Across town there is a knock at the door of the Davenport home. Malik walks from the living room to answer it. It's sweet, Scoot."

"Scoot, what's up, money?" says Malik. They embrace.

"Same old shit, but I need to speak with you on the for your ears only side," says Scooter.

"Come on in, Sakinah is out with Lenora and Kevin," says Malik. They both walk into the living room and take a seat. Sweet Scoot is half Puerto Rican, and half black. He's about Malik's height and size. Handsome with a warm smile. He's a street wise underground type, smartly dressed always, with all the angles on the street. "My brother, you're not going to believe this," says Scoot.

"Believe what?" Malik asks, moving to the edge of his seat.

"They have those bustas downtown."

"What bustas?" Malik asks.

"The bustas that shot your children, my brother. They got 'em."

Malik jumps to his feet searching for words. "Are you sure it's them?" he asks excitedly.

"I'm positive," says Scooter. "One of my girls, Tracy James works at the Blue Room, she called me and told me that the police rolled up in the joint and snatched them out the pool room earlier this evening."

"What station are they in?" Malik asks.

"The city, more than likely. They are being questioned right now. Next they will be charged, arraigned, and bail set. Then they will be moved to the county. That could take three to four days," says Scooter.

"Thanks, my brother. I owe you big time," says Malik.

Sweet Scoot stands and the two of them embrace again. "You don't owe me, bro, I owe you," says Scooter.

"Oh, by the way, Mark and Darren got in touch after they heard about the shorties, bruh. They say they're down for whatever."

"Mark and Darren?" Malik asks with a puzzled look.

"Yeah, Mark Wallington and Darren Black. They say that you all went to school together. They're out in California now."

Malik smiles. "Yeah, they're old friends. I just couldn't figure out how you would know them. I had misplaced their numbers?"

"My brother, not only do I have your back, but I'm international. I used to date Darren's sister Picsey Black. Don't think because I don't have as much melanin in my skin as you do that I don't have no soul," says Scooter.

They both smile then touch fist. "You've always had that Scoot... I love you," says Malik.

"I love you too, my brother," says Scooter.

"Tell Mark and Darren that the party hasn't started yet, but once it does, all my real friends are invited. Put them in touch with Amin, just in case my phones are monitored."

"Will do," says Scooter as they walk toward the front door.

"Hey, once the party does start, I need you to keep your ear to the ground, but I don't want you involved. I don't think we should be seen together until everything is over," says Malik.

"Let me worry about that," Scoot suggest.

"I insist, we need a middle man," says Malik.

"What about Karen Goodwin? She's working late tonight up at the city," says Scooter.

"Fine," says Malik. Scooter turns and heads down the steps, as Malik closes the door, and returns to his private office to make a call.

He dials Amin. Seconds later, Amin picks up. "As Salamu Alaikum. They have both of them down at the city. Yeah, I know, Sweet Scoot said in three to four days, so we have time. I'm heading down there right now to see if I can get a look at them and speak to Scoot's people, our insider, she'll know when those lames are scheduled to be moved and how. I'll shoot out there when I'm finish."

Malik hangs up the phone then picks up the photo of his son and daughter. "I sure do miss you two. Inshaallah, I will be joining you soon. My soul is tired." Malik puts the photo down, grabs his jacket and car keys then heads toward the front door. As he steps out he sees Sakinah, Lenora, and Kevin just arriving. Sakinah walks up to him, carrying an arm full of bags.

"Hey, you, where are you going this time of night?" she asks.

Kevin runs over and hands Malik a rapped package. He's smiling and excited. "I brought this for you!" He says.

Malik bends down taking the package from Kevin. "Thank you. Can I open it when I get back?" he asks.

"Yes," says Kevin.

"Okay, I'll be back in a little while." Malik kisses Kevin on the forehead then turns back to Sakinah.

"Honey, walk me to my car," he says.

Lenora comes over. "Here, hand me those, girl. I'll take them inside."

"Okay thanks," says Sakinah as she gives Lenora the bags she's carrying and Malik's gift from Kevin. She then walks over to Malik's car.

"They've caught the two guys," Malik says.

"What? When?" Sakinah says, stopping in her tracks.

"Scooter stopped by a little while ago. He said they're down town. I'm going to see if I can get a look at them."

"But why?" asks Sakinah.

"Because they took something from me they can never replace. I want them to see the man behind those lives," says Malik.

"You want me to fix dinner?" Sakinah asks.

"Only if you're hungry. After I leave there I'm going to see Amin. So I may be late getting back."

"I'll be up waiting for you. I love you," says Sakinah. She kisses him, then walks to the house. Malik gets into his car and back out the drive way. Sakinah stands there briefly then closes the door.

Amin, Nino, Monk, and Pup are at their hideaway. They've been joined by four more of their ex-Marines comrades. Terrible-T, the pretty boy of the group (so he thinks). He's medium-built, dark eyes, wavy black hair with a part on the side. Mr. Slim Goody. PasQually has arrived; he's the moral advocate of the group, the conscience next to Malik. If he's here someone is definitely wrong. He's five-foot-seven, medium build, with a strong jawline, wide shoulders, with big dark eyes. Ant-Head, he's six-foot-two, slim build, lithe like a world-class sprinter. His little round head and beady eyes are the reason for his name. Last, but not least, Cuddy. He's the radical of the bunch. The same height and size as PasQually, with light brown eyes, full lips, and a gangsta walk. He's not afraid of anything that can be killed. His love for this group is unmatched, and everyone else knows this, so he is somewhat catered to. He's also the youngest of the group.

"Listen up," Amin yells. "That was Malik, he said that they have the two shooters at the city jail. He's on his way there now and will be coming here when he leaves there."

"So does that mean we are about to set it off?" Ant-Head asks.

"I think so," says Amin.

"Terrible, did you and Monk get those vests?" Amin asks.

"Yeah, we got them and about twelve extra. Cuddy has them over at his room."

"They real nice too, not to heavy," says Cuddy.

"PasQually did you and Nino check on the cars and the van?" asks Amin.

"All that's covered, big brother. We can get the cars the night before, as long as we know they're going to be moved by morning."

"Malik is working on that. What about the explosives, Cuddy?" Amin asks.

"We have everything we need to make a 'explosive' getaway. If need be," says Cuddy as he slaps hands with Pup.

"Yeah, if they want to go to war, war it is!" yells Pup.

Everyone starts talking and joking among themselves. Amin interrupts them again. "Hold it down, listen. This is some serious shit. When they begin finding the bodies of these supremacist, all hell is going to break out. These clowns may be hated by the majority of society, but they're still white."

"That's right," says Cuddy.

"And Mr. Charlie, ain't gonna stand for whites being killed of no kind," Cuddy adds with a fake southern accent.

"The reality," says Amin, "is that this ain't gonna last and we may all die, cause without doubt, we can't hold this hill down for long." Amin looks at each one of them. "Sooner or later, we gonna be overrun," he says.

"I don't know why, but I don't really give a damn," says Terrible-T. "For some reason, I feel better about this than the war. Those Vietnamese never called me nigger, never spit on me, never lynched, beat or raped my people," he says.

"That's right, bro," says PasQually. "At least this time, we'll kill a real enemy, someone who has murdered millions of us simply because of the envy of our skin."

"Listen to this," says Monk. "I was finishing up this book right here last night." Monk shows everyone the cover. "It's called *Before the Mayflower* by Lerone Bennett Jr. Let me read this part to you: Southern bourbons seeking to eliminate the Black Federal presence in the south under Jin Crow murdered the Black Post Master and his family around 1:00 AM Tuesday morning, February 1898, in Lake City South Carolina. Torches were applied to the post office as well as the home. Back just within the light stood over one hundred white murders, Armed with pistols and shotguns. By the time the fire awakened the sleeping family, the post master, his wife, four daughters, a son and an infant at the breast. The Mob had begun firing into the home. Hundreds of bullet holes found their way easily past the thin boarding and into the body of the family living there. The post master was the first to reach the door, but he was shot dead within the threshold, taking several bullets into his face and body. The mother had the baby in her arms, and had reached the door over her husband's body when a bullet tore through the skull of the infant and it fell to the floor, along with its mother who had been shot several times. Two of the girls had their arms broken close to the shoulder and will probably lose their arms. The other two daughters and the young son were killed." Monk finishes then looks up at everyone. "Can you imagine their terror?" he asks. "Not just for the father, and mother awakened this way, both trying to get outside to try an put a end to this. To try and save the lives of their children. and the Terror in the children themselves hearing the sound of hundreds of gun shots and seeing their parents fall dead and each one of them shot and killed?"

"That's fucked up!" says Nino, clearly angry.

"IN THE BOOK," says Monk. "He goes on to say how white men became more sadistic. Lynching Black men, women, children and some white women. Many were burned at the stake, mutilated, hacked to pieces, and roasted over slow fires."

"This motherfucker is truly crazy man!" yells PasQually. "Most Blacks," says Monk as he continues. "Were lynched for testifying against whites, seeking a job, swearing, failing to say Mister to whites, disputing the price of a store item and trying to vote." Everyone sits there speechless after hearing all of what was said. Amin moves to stand in the middle of the group. "No matter what happens after this, they still may not wise up. But one thing is for sure. They gonna learn what it's like to die and mourn the dead!" Everyone stands, nodding their heads in agreement, embracing the magnitude of what's about to come. "They murdered my godbabies and destroyed my best friends life, for that they all must die," says Amin.

Malik has arrived down town at the city building. He gets out his car, then walks into the entry, past the closed offices, trying to find the clerk's office and Karen. He locates it finally and walks in. A slim red haired white woman in a bright yellow dress walks up to him.

"May I help you, sir?" she asks.

"Yes I'm looking for Karen Goodwin, please," says Malik.

"Oh, hold on, she's on the phone. Who shall I say is asking for her?" asks the clerk.

"Tell her it's Malik Davenport."

The clerk walks toward the back offices. Moments later, Karen comes out and opens the gate. "As Salamu Alaikum, Malik," she says.

Malik is taken by surprise by the greeting. "Wa Laikum As Salam. Are you Muslim?" he asks.

"Not yet, but I've been studying," says Karen.

"That's great. Scooter told me that you would be working late."

"Come on back to my office so that we can talk." Karen holds the gate open for Malik then leads him back to her office. Malik is very impressed by her appearance. Karen is by every sense of the word "Amazon." Long curly black hair, hazel oriental shaped eyes, sculptured facial features, tahijian tan skin and legs like Tina Turner. She's six feet, two and a half inches tall, with natural full cherry red lips.

"Have a seat," she says to Malik as she takes the one behind her desk. "I just got off the phone with Scooter, he told me what's up," says Karen.

"How do you feel about that?" Malik asks.

"Truthfully, I wish that I could kick their asses myself! Anyone that would kill children like that deserves whatever they get and if I can help them get it, it's my pleasure. After all, they've always assisted each other in killing us," says Karen.

Malik smiles. "I see you're not only a beautiful sister your strong and very well informed," he says.

Karen blushes. "Thank you, now what exactly do you need?" she asks.

"I need to know in advance, when they will be moved from here to the county. No later than the night before," says Malik.

"That's no problem," Karen says.

"Do you have a number I can reach you at or a pager?" she asks.

"Both," says Malik. He then hands her his card.

"Well, I won't take up any more of your time," says Malik, rising from his seat.

"It's no problem. I enjoy talking to a strong brother, even if it's only briefly," says Karen, smiling brightly.

Slowly they both head out the door of Karen's office, but she pauses.

"Oh, I almost forgot," she says, shaking her head in reflection. "They will be moving them in an unmarked van. They're trying to avoid attention," she says.

"Great!" says Malik, lost in his thoughts momentarily. "Maybe you and Scooter can come to dinner sometime at my home?" he suggests.

"I'd like that," says Karen.

"Okay then, well, As Salamu Alaikum," says Malik.

"Wa Laikum As Salam," Karen replies with a broad smile.

Malik turns and walks out the door, then down the hall toward the elevators. Once there he reads a posting stating that the jail is on the eleventh floor. He pushes the elevator button, the door opens and he steps inside. The door closes. Moments later, the door opens again. He walks out the elevator, then up to a uniformed guard behind a caged enclosure. "My name is Malik Davenport, I understand that you have the two people responsible for killing my children and I would like to see them," he says.

"Mr. Davenport, I don't think that's possible. Hold on a moment," says the officer before picking up the phone to dial a number. "Is the lieutenant still up here?" he asks. "Tell him Mr. Davenport is here and he wants to see the suspects. I'll tell him." The officer hangs up the phone, turning back to Malik. "Mr. Davenport, the lieutenant will be right out."

Moments pass by before Lieutenant Jackson walks out into the waiting area and up to Malik. "Mr. Davenport, it's good to see you again. How are you?" he asks.

"I'm doing okay. I'd do a lot better though if I could talk to those two," says Malik.

"I'm afraid as bad as I'd like to do that, being a father myself, regulations won't allow me to," says Jackson.

"I just want to ask them why they killed my children?" says Malik.

"I understand, Mr. Davenport," says the lieutenant. "But they are in our custody and though we may not like it we must protect them."

"Could I at least look at them?" Malik asks.

Jackson gazes at the officer, who shrugs his shoulders. "Okay, they're behind a two-way mirror, they can't see you," he says.

"Fine," says Malik. He then moves toward the door, but Lieutenant Jackson stops him.

"I need to pat you down first, Mr. Davenport, and ask you to remove everything out of your pockets," says Jackson.

"No problem." Malik empties his pockets, then Jackson pats him down. "If you'd follow me, they're this way." The lieutenant leads Malik back to the interrogation rooms. Malik looks in on Reckless first. "We believe that he done the shooting. We are testing the weapon we found on him for a match." Malik stares at him intensely. Memorizing him down to the last detail. "The other one is over here," says Jackson, directing Malik to the next room. "He owns the blue racing car with the stripes and the skull on the back." Malik looks Skull over the same way.

"Thank you, Lieutenant," says Malik. "I've seen enough." Malik then turns and walks out the door, through the gate and into a waiting elevator.

Back inside the jail, the lieutenant knocks on the door with Skull in it. Brooks steps out. "How's it going?" he asks.

"A couple more days of this and I believe he will give us information on the Davenport children and several other murders he witnessed," says Brooks. Agent Oliver steps out also. "He's saying now that he wants an attorney. That he's not saying anything else until he sees one."

"Fine, with the evidence we have, maybe his attorney will advise him to co-operate and avoid the death penalty," says Jackson.

"Okay, wrap it up, then take them both to their cells. But keep them separated."

Back on the street, Malik is on his car phone talking to Amin. "Yeah, bro, I had a good look at them both. Yes, I'm cool, but listen, there's been a change of plans. I'm going home to be with Sakinah. I met with Scooter's people and she told me that we have at least a couple days. Is everything ready? Okay. We'll tell everyone I'll get out there tomorrow Inshaalah. Love you too, bro." Malik hangs up the phone then glances at the photo of Eunique dangling down from his rearview mirror.

At the Davenport home, Sakinah is in the bathroom taking a candlelight bubble bath while listening to some soothing contemporary jazz. She's on the phone with Jada. "Everyone has called or either stopped by earlier," she says.

"Uncle Enskin and Uncle Ronnie called twice. Auntie Mary, Lynn, and Tiny called. Auntie Betty, Vodkie, Misha, and Uncle Bruce all called about twenty minutes ago Jada beeping in on each other. I'm exhausted! No Malik said he had somewhere to go and he'd be home late. I think he's holding up rather well. You know how much he loved his children, especially his daughter girl. I keep a close eye on him. Oh hold on, I think he just came in." She listens. "Malik! Is that you?" yells Sakinah.

"It's me!" says Malik.

"My husband is home, I'll call you tomorrow Inshallah, As Salamu Alaikum." Sakinah gets out the tub, puts on a bathrobe, then goes downstairs. Malik is sitting in his office. Sakinah walks in, stopping just inside the door.

"Are you okay?" she asks.

"I'm fine. Come over here," says Malik.

Sakinah walks over. Malik places her on his lap, hugs her, kisses her, then looks at her face. "I love you, I always have, and I always will," he says.

"I know," says Sakinah as she smiles and snuggles up to him. "Do you remember when we were living in East Baltimore with your grandmother on North Broadway?" asks Malik.

"Yes and you used to put your hand over my mouth when we made love," says Sakinah, smiling.

"Yeah, you were making way too much noise."

"It was your fault."

"Yeah. Sure," says Malik. They both laugh. "Remember how we would walk up across North Ave. and go to McDonald's for fish sandwiches and fries?" Malik asks.

"And you would always take a big bite out of my sandwich?" Sakinah lightly chokes his neck.

Malik laughs. "For some reason, yours always tasted better than mine. I believe one of your ex-boyfriends must have been in the back making my sandwich," he says.

Sakinah laughs. "Yeah, well all the waitresses must have been your girlfriends on the side because all they did was hover over you and bend over."

"What?" says Malik as he bursts out laughing. "They did not bend over in front of me."

"Yes, they did," says Sakinah.

"Did not!" says Malik.

"Well, at least you admit they hovered," says Sakinah.

"Possibly, but only because they were jealous that my woman was so fine." Malik rubs Sakinah's back.

"Yeah, right," she says then kisses him on the cheek.

"What about your old drunk boyfriend Jimmy?" Malik asks.

"He was not my boyfriend!" Sakinah slaps Malik upside the head.

"Yes, he was," says Malik. "I almost had to shoot him over you at that bar on Green Mount Ave."

"Well, you let me walk all the way home from downtown at the Harbor by myself," says Sakinah. "Because your girlfriend was down there," she pouts.

"That's not true. You were acting like the spoiled brat that you are because I turned around to look at a woman that had a nice outfit on," says Malik.

"You still let me walk home by myself," says Sakinah poking her bottom lip out.

"I didn't think that you would," he says.

"I did," says Sakinah.

"You're crazy, that's why I love you so much." Malik kisses her passionately. "You want to make some more babies?" he asks.

"Sure, I do and I want them to look just like their father," says Sakinah.

"Let's go upstairs," Malik suggests then scoops Sakinah up, kissing her again and again as he walks with her out the room.

It's the next morning. Skull is sitting in the holding pen waiting on his attorney. She walks in and introduces herself. "Hello, Mr. Henson. My name is Diane Shaw. I've been appointed to represent you this morning at your hearing."

Diane makes a small attempt to smile. Diane is a white, small-built young attorney, blond hair, green eyes, dressed in a tailored dark green suit, with matching two-inch heels.

"As you know you've been charged with capital murder. We will enter a not guilty plea and ask for bail," she says.

"What if I want to make a deal?" Skull asks. He looks haggard as if he was awake all night.

"Well, this hearing is not the time for that. Once you receive your formal indictment, we can speak with the district attorney and see what he is willing to do."

"Yeah, all right," Skull says dejected.

"I should tell you also, that I don't expect a reasonable bond on this kind of case, especially in front of Judge Hawkins."

"Judge Boris Hawkins?" Skull asks.

"No, his wife, Francis. Listen, I'll see you inside the courtroom," says Diane.

She steps out the room and runs into Reckless's attorney, Tony Davis, in the hallway. "Hi, Diane," says Tony, clearly surprised to see her.

"Tony, how are you?" she asks.

"Just barely holding on. I've been assigned to represent Mr. Meyer, a.k.a. Reckless," Tony says with a roll of his eyes. "I take it that you have the other?" he asks. Tony is a light-skinned black attorney one year out of law school. He's stocky built, with Asiatic features. He is very well groomed in a dark blue single breast suit.

"Yes, I do, Mr. Henson, a.k.a. Skull. He's already asking about a plea," says Diane.

"My client doesn't seem to grasp the seriousness of these charges. I believe we may have a shot at an insanity plea," says Tony.

"They both get my vote," says Diane.

The jailers bring Skull by the two attorneys, then Reckless. They both are then escorted into a side door leading inside the court room. Diane turns to Tony. "I guess we'd better get in there with our clients," she says. "After you." Tony smiles, then steps aside to allow Diane to enter the courtroom first.

They each walk over and take a seat next to the defendants. Moments later, the judge's chamber doors opens, the bailiff then orders everyone to rise. The judge enters the court room taking her seat on the bench. "Be seated," she orders. Judge Hawkins looks over her paperwork, then out into the court. Judge Francis Hawkins has a reputation for being stern, but fair. A small black woman, who raised three sons and three daughters while putting herself through law school in the segregated south. She is very much respected and loved among her peers. "We have two complaints here. The charge is murder one, the State is Alabama vs. Michael Meyer and James Henson. Who do we have representing the State?" she asks.

"Kathy Campbell representing the State, your honor," says the strikingly beautiful young district attorney.

"And the defendants?" the judge asks.

"Diane Shaw representing Mr. Henson, your honor."

"Any pleads?"

"Yes, your honor," Diane says. "On behalf of Mr. Henson, we acknowledge receipt of the complaint, waive, its reading, enter a plea of not guilty and request bail be set."

"So noted," says Judge Hawkins. "Mr. Davis?" The Judge glares at the young attorney.

He fumbles, dropping his note pad as he stands. "Uh, your honor, on behalf of my client, Mr. Meyer, I also acknowledge receipt of the complaint, waive its reading enter a plea of not guilty and request bail," says Tony, who then retakes his seat.

"So noted, Ms. Campbell, does the State have recommendations regarding bail?"

"Yes, your honor," says the junior district attorney. "The State believes that these two are responsible for the murder of the Davenport children, as well as several federal armed robberies, with related murders. Neither of the two have a home address, employment, and the State believes that they are a flight risks."

The judge looks over at the defendants' table.

"Ms. Shaw?" Diane stands.

"Nothing, your honor," she says.

"Mr. Davis?" Tony stands.

"Nothing, your honor."

"Okay then, bail will be set for each of the defendants at one million dollars. They are to be remanded back to the custody of the sheriff, to wait transfer to the county jail. This count is adjourned!" Judge Hawkins slams her gravel down then exits the bench. The deputies step up and take the defendants out one by one. Reckless is trying to get Skull's attention, but Skull keeps his head down. Attorney Davis watches him then turns to Diane. "I sure hope my client takes a deal, this is one case I don't want anything to do with," he says.

"I believe it's an open-shut case," says Diane. "I've been told that a friend of the children seen my client's car pull up behind the kids and that your client climbed into the back seat and shot them."

Diane begins placing her papers back into her briefcase. "Wow!" says Tony. "Let's just pray for a miracle," he suggests.

"We are going to need one," says Diane. They both pick up their brief cases then head out the door.

CHAPTER 8

It's late evening and Malik is in the kitchen getting something out of the refrigerator when the phone rings.

"Hello," he says. "Oh, Wa Lakum As Salam Karen, how are you? That's good, okay, tomorrow, do you have any idea what time? Between eight and ten. Shukran! Oh, that means thank you. Okay, As Salamu Alaikum." Malik hangs up the phone then rushes upstairs to change clothes.

Sakinah sees him come into the room. She turns the volume down on the television, before sitting up in bed. "Are you going somewhere?" she asks.

"I've got to go see Amin, I may not be back until tomorrow sometime, so if anyone calls or comes by before I return, tell them I am resting, and I do not want to be disturbed." Sakinah gets out of the bed and walks over to where Malik is standing. "Malik, I never question you about the decisions you make because I love you and I trust you to lead and to protect our family. I'm not going to worry you about anything because I don't want to distract you. But I will say this." Sakinah pauses, taking both Malik's hands into hers. "Whatever you are about to do, use your head, and I'll see you tomorrow, God willing."

Malik pulls her to him, hugging, then kissing her softly. "I love you, baby, and I will." Malik turns back to getting dressed. He opens one of the closet doors and removes a brown duffel bag, a black quarter-length leather coat, and black gloves before leaving the room and heading out to his car.

Amin has hung up the phone after speaking to Malik. He turns to speak to the members of "Faze Two" that are present. "Malik is on his way. He says the good old boys are going to be moved tomorrow morning between eight and ten. So we need to move everything to the safe house in town so that we can be ready first thing in the morning."

"I'll bring the van around so we can load it up," says Pup.

"Why don't you have Malik just meet us at the safe house?" asks Nino.

"Malik says that he wants to speak to everyone first," says Amin.

"We all know what that is about," says Terrible-T. They all glance at each other shaking their heads knowing why Malik is coming.

Detectives Brooks and Taylor, along with Agents Oliver and Branch are sitting in a conference room going over articles they have taken from Skull's car and other information they've compiled. "At the moment, we have not come across anything linking them to any specific racial group," says Branch.

"Does that lessen your theory of another spree of child murders?" asks Brooks.

"Not at all," says Branch. "We still have no known address on these two and they have no legit source of income that we know of yet. They appear to be able to bounce from town to town as they please."

"So someone is providing for their travel expenses?" asks Taylor.

"And women," says Branch.

"Has the lab reported back on the gun yet?" Oliver asks.

"No," says Taylor.

"But they promised me that they would have the report finished by tomorrow."

"Good," says Oliver.

"Because we also want to test it up against slugs taken from two victims from Bank robberies in Mississippi."

"Judge Hawkins gave them a million-dollar bond. Any chance someone will spring them?" Brooks asks.

"It's possible," says Branch. "Especially if their associates believe that they may be spilling their guts."

"Shit, they probably already know that ole Skull is kinda soft in spirit," says Oliver. They all laugh at the thought.

Malik has just arrived at Amin's. He gets out of his car, then walks into the house. Everyone calls his name then stands as Malik greets each one of them warmly with a firm hand shake and embrace. "Old friends," says Malik. "Before we leave, I just want to say that I love all of you for your support over all the years. We have faced many battles together, but this one is mine, and I understand it if anyone here does not want to be a part of this. You all have your own lives to live, and—"

Amin interrupts him, "Shut up!" Amin pushes Malik playfully up against the wall."

"You see," says Terrible-T. "I told ya'll that he was coming out here with some bullshit." They all laugh.

"Blood in, blood out, bro, ain't no turning back now," says Monk.

"Yeah, we all know what it is, and believe me, this should have been done a long time ago," says Cuddy.

"Can we get going now?" asks Nino.

"Sure, baby boy," says Malik.

Everyone picks up their gear and begin heading out to the van. Malik taps Amin on the shoulder and asks him to ride with him. Once inside the car, Amin turns to Malik. "Did you speak with Sakinah?" he asks.

"Not really, I just told her I'm not to be disturbed until tomorrow night if someone calls on comes by."

"Is she cool with that?"

"Yes, she's good," says Malik.

"So what do you want to do with these two if things go right?" Amin asks.

"I'd rather not speak on that right now, Amin, let's just enjoy the night Bruh like we used to do before we'd go into battle," Malik suggests.

"True that!" says Amin.

Back at the Davenport residence, Ms. Norma is knocking on the door. She waits a brief moment before Sakinah opens the door. "Hi, Mom," says Sakinah with a smile and a kiss on Ms. Norma's cheek.

"Hi, baby."

"Come on in," says Sakinah, stepping back to allow her mother-in-law to enter the foyer before closing the door. "I just thought I'd stop by to see how you two were doing. Where is he?" asks Ms. Norma.

"He's resting," says Sakinah. "He said that he was very tired."

Ms. Norma walks into the living room and takes a seat. "Good," she says. "He needs some rest, where is he upstairs?"

"Yes, ma'am."

"He isn't sick, is he?" asks Ms. Norma.

"No, just tired."

"Well, when do you want to start sorting out some of the children's things. Most of them I think you should keep so that you can give them to their future brothers and sisters," says Ms. Norma with a smile. Sakinah also smiles at the thought.

Across town, Malik and his comrades have made it to the safe house. Its owner, Hasheem Willie Carter III, comes out to greet them. Hasheem is a bear of a man, and a gifted gentle giant, with deep roots in Chicago and the motor city. He was not a part of Faze Two, choosing instead to serve with the Navy. He and Malik met by chance and discovered that they had mutual friends in both cities, and in the Moorish Science Temple where Hasheem was at one time the Grand Sheike. Hasheem is about six-feet-four, two hundred and fifty pounds solid. He is athletic, and a natural poet.

He walks out on the porch, then down the steps to greet Malik. "My beloved brother, Islam," says Hasheem.

"Islam my brother, it's been way too long Hasheem," says Malik as the two of them embrace tightly.

"Ever since you became a corporate lawyer you have been hard to locate," says Hasheem with a smile. "I'm going to change that, bro," says Malik.

"Everyone, come on in," says Hasheem as one by one he embraces them as they pass on their way inside with their gear. Once inside, Malik stands by Hasheem and introduces him. "My brothers, this is Hasheem, we go a long way back." They all say what's up. He then turns to Hasheem. "Bruh, this is Pasqually, Monk, Cuddy, Ant-Head, Pup, Terrible-T, and my cousin Nino."

"It's a pleasure to meet all of you, I know ya'll have to be solid because that's the only way Malik rolls. So all of you take a load off and make yourselves at home."

"I hope you don't mind, but we brought our own party in our bags. Amin and Malik do not drink," says Pup.

"Neither do I," says Hasheem. "But for those of you who do, the glasses are in the kitchen." Cuddy goes for the glasses while everyone else piles into the living room where Jazz is playing low over the stereo.

Nino pulls out a couple of ounces of Gold Weed and begins rolling up joints. "Now I know you squares are not going to say no to this Bud all the way from Indonesia," he says.

"I'm not," says Ant-Head.

"Let me help you with that." Cuddy returns with several glasses and two bottles of liquor and stands in the middle of the room.

"I've got rum, and I've got gin to make your blood thin in hopes that you'll win in the end." Everyone smiles and laughs.

"Hey, you all remember our rum and Coke song we sung around the campfire?" asks Pasqually.

"I do!" says Cuddy excitedly as he begins popping his fingers, then begins the song. "Coke adds life to what the real life is all about." Everyone joins in. "Gonna start a little bit more, Mary Jane and Billy Bob, sitting sue and snozzy too, shu, be, do, be, do, aa, da-da." Everyone cracks up laughing at their silliness. "Say, Malik, you remember when we were out in the Mojave Desert and that staff sergeant left you on that lookout point for three days with one days supply of food and water," asks Terrible-T.

"Yes, I remember that."

"Boy you were smoking," says Pup.

"You came into the tent without saying a word and tossed your M-16, Pistol, Cripto Gear and everything else on the ground. That shit was too funny!"

"Yeah," says Amin.

"Then he grabbed his civilian clothes then thumbed a ride to Los Angeles for four days."

"That was a classic," says Ant-Head, as he reaches over to blow Cuddy a toke.

"And the battalion commander didn't even court martial his ass once he found out what happened," says Pasqually.

"That's because Malik kept his nose up his ass," says Pup.

"That's because I done a damn good job setting up his communication network," says Malik.

Terrible-T takes a long drag on the joint then passes it to Hasheem. "What about when you beat up that racist staff sergeant, the one that wore the KKK ring, I forgot his name."

"Up in Bridgeport California?" asks Malik.

"Yes, that's the one," says Amin. "He called me out."

"You could have refused," says Cuddy, smiling. "And I never would have heard the last of it from you cowards!" Malik smiles at the thought. "Don't forget also that when he barged into our tent ordering us out to unload the pallets, that while I continued to take my clothes off, all of you began putting yours on."

"Everyone is not afraid of a lil hard work," says Amin.

"Me neither, but you all know why he came to our tent," says Malik.

"Sure we do," says Monk.

"He'd gotten word that you had mauled his buddy while we were in the Mojave. He didn't like that."

"Imagine this little private refusing to work when the order was racist, beating up staff NCOs and the battalion commander loves him," says Amin.

"The master gunny sergeant did also," says Ant-Head.

"Remember when he called that Battallion Formation at nine thirty at night after Malik kicked the staff sergeant over the cliff," Amin asks.

"Yeah, and all he said was, 'Get rid of that chip on your shoulder,'" says Pup as they all burst out laughing.

"Yeah, fuck that you just kicked a staff sergeant down a two hundred yard cliff," says Nino. They all laugh even harder, then suddenly everyone stops and it's quiet. Amin walks over to Malik.

"Yeah, and that's why we all here, bro, 'cause you are real like that. You done the shit we all wanted to do. Everything you fought, every one of us had it better because of it, you know."

"Mom says I came out of her womb like that, she says it's why my granny named me Pappi," says Malik.

"Pappi." Laughs Cuddy.

"What kind of shit is that?" They all burst out laughing again.

"Pappi," says Ant-Head.

"Damn!" everyone laughs some more. "Hey, take that sad shit off Hasheem, you got any funkadelic?" asks Cuddy.

"Aint no question," says Hasheem.

He walks over to his album collection and pulls out "Mother Ship Connection" then places it on the turn table. Suddenly everyone is up dancing and singing!"

"If you hear any noise it's just me and the boys, hit me!"

It's early morning just before dawn and Malik and Amin are sitting in a Midnight Blue 1976 GTO...Terrible-T and Nino are in a Black 1975 Electra 225 right across the street one parking lot away from the intersection. Pasqually is standing on the corner dressed as a homeless man with explosives under his jacket. "What time is it?" Amin asks.

"Nine thirty," says Malik.

"They are running late," says Amin.

"Not really," says Malik as Pasqually signals to him.

"Here they come," he says as he blows his horn twice. Terrible and Nino both see the van... Terrible pulls out in front of it then stops. As the van passes by Malik, he pulls up behind it. Terrible backs up as Malik closes in behind the van, then he and Amin jump out with AR 15s in their hands. Nino and Terrible do the same.

"Hands on the dash, let me see your hands now!" orders Malik.

"Open up the damn door before I start blasting," screams Nino. The deputies are terrified!

"Okay, whatever you say," says the chubby deputy on the passenger side.

"Get your ass out now!" screams Terrible-T as he takes a shooting stance and points his weapon at the guards head. The passenger's side deputy opens the door and Terrible-T snatches him out the van placing him face-down on the ground. Nino jerks the driver out of his seat over the console, then out the passenger side door and places him face down also on the ground, cuffing them both from behind. Terrible takes the keys and opens the side door to where the two prisoner are being kept.

"Motherfuckers, get the fuck out, you two are coming with us!" he screams.

"This is against the law!" yells Reckless.

"What's going on!" screams Skull. "What do you guys want?"

Amin walks up and slaps skull in the mouth with so much force that he spits out a couple teeth and a mouth full of blood. Nino helps Terrible get them into the trunk of the first car, while Malik takes the deputies gun and the ignition key to the van. He turns to Amin.

"Kill that radio!" he orders.

Amin smashes it. "We are out of here!" says Malik.

He and Amin jump back into the GTO pulling around the van, following Terrible and Nino. A few blocks away they spot Pup, Monk, and Cuddy sitting in an alley in the floral van waiting. They all pull up, Nino and Terrible snatch Skull and Reckless out of the trunk of the car, then drag them over to the van as Cuddy slides the door open. "I see we have guest," says Cuddy as he slams his hand gun into Reckless's face, before pulling him into the van. Both Reckless and Skull are terrified out of their minds. They can hardly speak. Nino, Terrible, and Amin jump in behind them as Malik peeps into the van at the two responsible for killing his children.

"I'll see you all in a few days, as soon as I know it's clear. Take care of them." Malik slides the van door closed, before walking over to his Jaguar, getting in and heading home. Several blocks away Pasqually is seen standing in line to get on the bus. The deputies have run over to the phone on the corner to call the station but they discover someone has snatched the cord out.

The van with Amin and the boys is seen on the road heading out of town. "You good old boys are in a lot of trouble," says Pup with a cold smile. Cuddy turns in his seat so that Reckless and Skull can see him sharpening the blade on his twelve-inch hunting knife.

"It wasn't me, man!" screams Skull.

"He did it, I told him not to."

"Shut the fuck up!" screams Reckless.

"I didn't do a damn thing, that lying coward done it. He drove me over there, shit, it's his car!" Nino smacks them both.

"Shut the fuck up, you pieces of shit! We are going to make sure the both of you die slow. We already know who done what."

"Those two children you killed were my Godbabies," says Amin.

"I was there when they both come into this world. I was there when they learned to walk, to talk and I promised their father, that as Godfather I would protect them with my life. What you done has made a liar out of me, and for that and what you have done, make no mistake about it, you are going to die a very painful death," Skull begins to shiver and shake uncontrollably.

Malik is pulling up in his driveway. He gets out of his car then walks up to his front door where he finds his mother standing. "Hi, Mom," he says before kissing her on the cheek. "I thought you were upstairs asleep," she says.

"I snuck out earlier, I had to go by and see Mike Latimore." "You want something to eat?"

"No, Ma, not right now, where is Sakinah?" Malik asks.

"She's upstairs." Malik walks in and gives her a kiss. "She spent the night, there was nothing I could do."

"Don't worry about it, I'm going to take a shower." Malik peels his sweater off as he heads into his bedroom.

Across town police, sheriffs, Taylor, Brooks, Agents Branch, Oliver, Captain Twyman, Lieutenant Jackson, and a large crowd of reporters and spectators are on the scene of the snatch. "Who were they?" asks Captain Twyman.

"They had on Halloween masks, we didn't see their faces, they also had on gloves," says the sheriff's van driver.

"Did you get a look at the cars?" asks Captain Twyman.

"Yes," says the van driver.

"We already called it in."

"How many were there?" Taylor asks.

"Four, I think," says the passenger side sheriff, who appears still very shaken. A patrolman walks up to the captain.

"Sir, they found both of the cars four blocks from here."

"Get a team over there right now, I want every inch of those cars gone over, do you hear me?"

"Yes, sir," says the officer before heading off.

"Captain, we were just discussing last night the possibility that the organization that those two are associated with might try to free them," says Branch.

"Why would they?" the captain asks.

"Because those two may have information of murders or murder plots they do not want anyone knowing about," says Brooks.

"Someone is financing them, that's for sure, they have nothing, and they are not smart enough to operate on their own," says Branch. Another police officer walks over to speak with the captain. "Captain, you are wanted on the radio."

Twyman takes the radio from the officer clearly frustrated over all that's taken place. "This is Captain Twyman. Yes, are you sure, fine, file the report, I'll get back with you once I'm back on station." The captain returns the radio back to the officer before turning back to his detectives and the FBI agents. "That was Ballistics, the gun that you found on Meyers matched the bullet's that killed the Davenport children."

"Damn!" says Taylor.

"Well, looks like we have work to do," says Oliver.

"Kidnapping is a federal crime, we need to report back to our supervisor and give him the details."

"Kidnapping!" shouts Brooks.

"This was an escape!"

"Maybe," says Oliver. "Maybe not. But until we get more information, I suggest we keep all avenues open, that way we broaden our scope and resources."

"I think that is a good idea," says Captain Twyman.

"We can use all the help that we can get on this. Taylor, I want you to assign officers to talk with anyone that may have seen what took place here from those buildings across the street. Check the bus schedule also, maybe someone waiting at the stop over there seen something."

"I'm on it," says Taylor.

"Agents Branch, Oliver I'd like for you to make a joint statement with me to the press concerning the background on these two. I believe that members of their organization freeing them is more plausible, so let's go with that."

"Fine with me," says Oliver.

"Me too," says Branch. Captain Twyman, Branch and Oliver walk over to where a large group of reporters are being held back and give them the story.

Attorney Tony Davis and Diane Shaw are having lunch together sitting at the bar talking politics when the news story of their clients escape is broad casted.

"What the hell!" says Tony, spitting half of his Long Island iced tea back into the glass.

"Oh shit!" says Diane.

"There is your miracle, there is a God after all." The lawyers quickly finish off their drinks, drop money down for the cost, grab their briefcases, then rush out the door.

Karen Goodwin is sitting in her office when one of the clerks that works with her, runs into her office to share the news. "Girl, you know those two they arrested for killing those two children?" asked the clerk excitedly.

"Yes. What about them?" asks Karen.

"Some of their friends hi-jacked the van about an hour ago and rescued them!"

"Was anyone hurt?" asks Karen.

"No, I don't think so."

"Okay, thanks for letting me know. Would you excuse me. I need to make an important phone call."

"Sure," says the clerk, before rushing out the room to tell anyone else that missed the special report. After the door closes Karen sits back in her chair smiling to herself. "Malik, you're one bad brother," she says. She then picks up her phone and dials a number and waits. "Hi, sweet Scoot. Everything is good, so when can I get that dinner you promised me?"

Ms. Norma and Sakinah are watching the news report in the kitchen as Sakinah finishes off the last of the dishes from lunch… She calls Malik into the room, where the three of them watch the broadcast in silence. Ms. Norma looks over at her son and so does Sakinah. "Come over here Malik, and sit down with me baby," says Ms. Norma. She places one of the bar stools directly in front of her and Malik takes a seat. Ms. Norma looks him directly in his eyes for a moment before taking his hands in hers and kissing them. "I hope you know what you are doing sweetheart and what it might cost," she says.

"Mom, I—"

Ms. Norma cuts him off. "Shh. I taught you to fight back when someone hits you. So do you think that I didn't live with the possibility that someone might end up hurting you because you wouldn't retreat? I allowed you to fight for America, so what can I say when you've decided to fight for what's yours." Ms. Norma kisses Malik's hands again before getting up and leaving the room. Sakinah walks over and takes her seat.

"I want to see them," she says.

"No!" says Malik. "I gave birth to Kazi and Eunique. I carried them inside my body for nine months. I have a right to see them. To see the people that took my creation away from me, Malik."

Malik nods his head slightly, pausing to take in all Sakinah has said. "Sweetheart, love of my life, do you understand what is going on here fully. Do you? This is not a game, this is kidnapping and murder. We could lose everything including our lives in the electric chair."

"I've lost half of everything that gave my life meaning anyways, I don't care."

Malik studies his wife even deeper before responding. "Listen, no matter what happens to me, you have to go on, you and Mom."

"I don't want to hear that, Malik."

"Listen, Sakinah! I don't want you involved in this, I don't think I'm making it through this. I have a feeling, that's all. But you've got to be strong. If I don't stand up against this racial oppression, who is going to do it baby? There are no more Nat Turners, Malcox X's, Meagan Evers, and so many others. Brothers and sisters that willingly put their lives at risk for real freedom and change. They're all gone baby, and they left behind wives, children, mothers and family. Seemingly our fighting spirit as a people left with them."

"I just have one question, Malik, why you?"

"I don't know, I'm drawn to this, it's spiritual. I hate the thought of innocent people being hunted down like their animals, lynched, and set on fire. While these groups of people sit around laughing at the terror they have caused, as if there is humor in loss of life. I'm commanded by the creator as a man to stand up for the weak and oppressed. If I don't then I'm just as worthless as all these other men who witnessed women, children, and the elderly murdered in unspeakable ways all over the world and responded with silent cowardliness or by singing songs about overcoming in the future—not today. I'm sick of seeing that shit, Sakinah! Maybe just maybe, this will help break the chain of fear in my nation and our youth and those to come, will grow up fearless instead of inheriting the cowardly response to the murder of our people by racist whites that they see in so many black men today."

Sakinah wipes away a tear then kisses Malik softly on his lips. "Okay," she says, before standing up and leaving the kitchen also.

Malik picks up the phone on the counter then dials Amin. Moments later, he picks up. "Did you see the news report?" Malik asks.

"I never thought of it from that point of view. Maybe heaven is smiling on us, bro. I'll be out there tonight. Salam." Malik completes the call then dials another number.

"Can I speak to Hugh Lament please. Tell him it's Malik." Malik is placed on hold briefly before Hugh Lamont comes on the line.

"What's up?" says Malik. "Look, did you think about that information I told you I needed. I need an answer by the weekend. If you have something for me, drop it off Saturday evening," says Malik before hanging up the phone abruptly.

Agents Branch and Oliver are at FBI Headquarters sitting in Chief Clarence Jacock's office. "So the plot thickens," says the chief.

"John and I believe that these two were rescued by members of their group, or kidnapped," says Oliver.

"Kidnapped! Who would want to kidnap them?" asks the chief.

Agents Branch and Oliver glance at each other, but say nothing. "Did the deputies get any kind of ID on them?"

"No, they wore Halloween masks and gloves," says Branch. "Well, what about the sound of their voices any ethnic clue there?"

"Nothing on that either," says Branch.

"Okay, what about the vehicles?"

"Chief, they were both stolen sometime early morning," says Oliver.

"So these boys knew their stuff, huh?"

"I'm thinking they had military training," Oliver suggests.

"That won't help. All these Supremacy groups use U.S. Military Training Manuals," says Branch.

"So basically until someone comes forward with a lead on the suspects or the people that took them, we have nothing to go on?" the chief asks.

"That's about it," says Branch.

"I'm thinking we should do a run down on friends and known associates of Mr. Reckless and Skull, perhaps some of them are hiding them, or knows who is," suggests Oliver.

"Well, that's better than just sitting on our ass," says Chief Jacocks.

Agents Branch smiles at the chief. "You think perhaps we could come up with a few search warrants to look into the closets of some of these known associated?" he asks.

"The name Clarence Jacocks still carries a little clout over at the US Attorney General's Office. I'll see what I can do."

CHAPTER 9

It's close to midnight, and Malik is walking into a shed which has been used as the holding location for the murderers of his children. Both captives are tied up tight and gagged. Amin is leading the way. Nino, Pup, Cuddy, Pasqually, Monk and Terrible-T are already inside. They snap to attention when they see Malik.

"Well, boys, it's judgement day," says Pup.

Both Reckless and Skull have had large swastikas carved into the middle of their foreheads. Cuddy sits directly across from them sharpening his twelve-inch bo-knife. At their feet sits a small tin bucket, full of teeth; the two captives have had every tooth in their mouth torn out, their ears have been cut off, and both thumbs. Malik is wearing his 45-caliber handgun with the white pearl hand grip in his shoulder holster. Both Reckless and Skull's eyes bulge at the sight of it.

"Take the gags out their mouths," orders Malik.

Nino and Monk snatch them off. "I promised the mother of the children you murdered, my wife, that I would ask you why you done what you did. For her."

"I didn't do it, man, he did it. I told him not to but he wouldn't listen. I swear to God, it wasn't me!" screams Skull.

"That fucker is lying, man, to save his own ass, he did it, he drove me there, it was his car!" yells Reckless.

"Shut up!" shouts Malik.

"You're right, he drove and you climbed in the back seat and shot my son, then my daughter. You slaughtered them. Babies!" Malik is shaking with rage.

"It wasn't me, please, I'm begging you, don't do this man!" yells Reckless. "Put their gags back in their mouths, I've heard enough," says Malik as he begins to pace back and forth in front of Skull and Reckless. "I've searched my soul and mind over and over. I've asked myself repeatedly why are you doing this and does this place me on a level with you? A lot of people believe that is the case, it's why very few have hit back when struck by your kind. Finally I asked myself, is it possible to make a moral plea, to the immoral. I don't think it's possible, my people have struggled to do so for over four hundred years, with no success. It's time for you to die!"

In a flash, Malik pulls his handgun from the holster and shoot's both Skull and Reckless twice each in the face and head. They both fall over dead.

"Damn!" screams Cuddy.

"Burn that trash," says Malik before walking out the door, Amin right behind him. "Are you okay, bruh?"

Malik turns around, he's crying. He and Amin embrace. "I know, bro, I know," says Amin.

"There is no turning back now," says Malik.

"Not until it's over one way or the other," says Amin.

"Hugh Lamont may have what we need, Saturday, I'll let you know. You got this?" asks Malik.

"Yeah, you go on home and try to get some rest."

It's Saturday afternoon. Malik is sitting out by the swimming pool reading the paper when Kevin runs out to him. "Hey, little man!" says Malik, taken by surprise.

"Hey, Malik!" says Kevin shyly.

"What's up?" Malik asks.

"You said you would take me to the fair. It's Saturday."

"All ready?" says Malik playfully.

"Yes," says Kevin as his mother walks over to where her son is standing. "As Salamu Alaikum Malik, I told him that this was not a good time, that you were busy," says Lenora. "No, I don't have anything planned until later on tonight, not only that, but when a man gives his word, he must honor that always right Kev?"

"Yes, sir," says Kevin.

"See, Mom, I told you, he wants to take me."

"I sure do, let me change clothes and shoes right quick, come on Kev." Malik reaches out and takes Kevin's hand as they walk back into the house. Lenora stands there so grateful for the love and attention Malik gives to her only child.

Across town, Jada, Raquel, Kathy, Janice, Aunt Barbara, Aunt Catherine, and Uncle Bruce, are all sitting around the dinner table at aunt Pat's home, discussing the kidnapping of the white supremacist. "Listen, I think some of their friends helped them and their on the way out the country or up into the mountains somewhere," says Aunt Bob.

"I agree," says Uncle Bruce. "I don't think they would stay around here, I know I wouldn't," says Raquel.

"Hell, no one seen what they looked like, they all had on masks," says Kathy.

"That's what I'm saying," says Jada.

"If the people who took them were their buddies, why didn't they kill the police. After all, that's what they do, right?" asks Jada.

Aunt Pat and Jada lock eyes briefly then Aunt Pat stands up suddenly. "I have some unfinished work at the office that I need to complete before Monday morning. I should be back home around eight." Aunt Pat picks up her brief case then turns and walks out the door.

It's early evening. Malik is at the carnival with Kevin. He's holding a large stuffed Snoopy dog that he has won for Kevin. Kevin has his cotton candy and Malik has a caramel apple. They try a couple games together. They ride the spinning tops, the fairest wheel, the bumper cars, the flying airplanes, all before walking over to get hot dogs, curly fries, lemonade, then taking a seat at one of the many picnic tables. They are having a lot of fun.

"Wow!" says Kevin. "I like driving, Malik!"

"You are a good driver Kev, it won't be long now and you will be going to get your license."

"Really! When it's time will you teach me to drive a real car, Malik!"

"Sure I will, and I'll even buy you the first one."

"You will!" Kevin is excited.

"Sure, it may not be brand-new, but it will be nice and reliable."

"Wait until I tell mom!" Kevin stuffs a handful of curly fries into his mouth, then washes it down with a big gulp of lemonade.

"Thanks, Malik."

"I told you, Kev, anytime you want something, just let me know okay."

Kevin sits there a moment in silence.

"Malik."

"Yes, Kevin?"

"I really miss Kazi and Eunique. They were the only sister and brother I had."

"I know, Kev, they miss you too. Now eat your food so that we can try one more ride before we leave."

"Can we get back into the cars!"

"If that's what you want."

"Yeeaa!" says Kevin. Malik sits back and watches Kevin enjoy his food.

Aunt Pat is at her office on the phone with her sister, Ms. Norma. "Norma, you know Malik is like my own son, now if he is in any kind of trouble, I want to know about it. No I'm not saying that he is. I'm just worried. I'm finishing up here in about an hour, then I'm going to see him. Okay, I'll tell him." Aunt Pat hangs up the phone then sits back in her chair lost in thought.

It's late evening. Malik is home from the fair, sitting in his study looking at slides of his children doing a variety of different things when Sakinah walks in. "Malik, Hugh Lamont is here."

"Tell him to come in here." Sakinah walks into the hallway where Hugh is hanging up his jacket.

"What's in the envelope?" Sakinah asks.

"Just some paperwork for Malik."

"So where have you been I haven't seen nor heard from you in a few days?"

"I've been busy at work, thinking about a lot of different things."

"So why is it that you and Malik are suddenly constantly in contact with each other?"

"We are not constantly in contact with each other, he just asked me to help him get some information and I did, that's it. Listen, I don't have to explain nothing to you little sister."

"Then don't, Malik is in his study," says Sakinah before stepping aside allowing Hugh Lamont to pass and to walk into the study where he finds Malik sitting in the darkened room watching his children. "Come on in and close the door."

Hugh Lamont closes it but remains standing by it. "You see that photo right there, it was taken the day I brought Kazi home."

"I remember."

"That one was taken seven days after his birth, when I held him up before the Heavens and his ancestors and bore witness that he lived, the son of Malik, the son of Norma Jean, daughter of Ruth and Enise Bell, Ruth, the daughter if Dossi and Judge Graham. And there is Eunique, look at the sparkle in her eyes. She had her mother's eyes. That's her in the bathtub with me. Somehow she always knew when I was getting in the tub and she would run and jump in without taking off her clothes."

Malik laughs at the memory and shakes his head. "She would say, 'More bubbles please!' "Sakinah would have a fit! I swear, it was so cute." Lamont interrupts Malik, he steps forward with the envelope, placing it on the table. "I have here what you asked for. You want to tell me now what you want with this?"

"No, but I will anyway, I'm going after WHITE SUPREMACY."

"You are what!" Lamont is taken by surprise.

"Yes, they are so comfortable with destroying other people's lives, that they have never ever considered how it would feel having the same things done to them."

"You are crazy!" shouts Hugh Lamont.

"Don't you call me crazy you sniveling coward, look at that!" shouts Malik, jumping to his feet. He pulls up a slide of black men hung by their necks from a tree.

"And that!" A slide of Emmitt Till lying in his coffin with his face swollen grotesquely and broken. "He was murdered, beaten to death, because he allegedly whistles at a white woman. He was a young kid only fourteen years old. His murderers bragged and made jokes about the way they kidnapped and beat him, then tied a cotton fan around his neck before tossing him into the river. They never did a day in prison, they were found not guilty by an all-white jury. Look at that."

Slides of more black men lynched and hanging from a tree. "That, my man, is crazy!" screams Malik.

"But what's more insane, is that we have allowed it to happen for years, all over the country. Can you imagine what our ancestors who died like this think of us. How can they rest knowing there are no men left among us?"

"You could be killed," Hugh Lamont suggests.

"I recall Nat Turner saying that he had a divine vision that called for him to rise up, even Moses was divinely inspired to break the cycle of bondage."

"Have you been spoken to by God?" Hugh asks sarcastically.

"I believe so, I believe that my call came with the death of my children, the Creator knew that their death would compel me to fight." Malik turns and walks back behind his desk retaking his seat. "And what about my sister?" Hugh asks. "My wife understands me very well."

"I don't want to have anything else to do with this," yells Hugh Lamont. "You and the other knee grows like you, get out!" orders Malik. Hugh opens the door to leave but pauses just long enough to see Malik go back to the slide of Emmitt Till laying in his coffin. He then closes the door.

It's very early Sunday morning, the sun is rising on what looks to be a very pleasant mild sunny day in Mobile. Malik is at Amin's place going over the locations of the Supremacy groups in the Mobile area. Terrible is sitting there also with a map full of multicolored sticks pins. "So the pins with the white heads are Aryans, the ones with pink are klans men?" Terrible asks.

"That's correct," says Amin.

"Okay, we have about eight Klan groups, and six Aryans is our area?"

"Yes, and the red pin heads indicate the locations of the leaders of each group," says Amin.

"Good! That's where we will start first, see how these groups are to the south and the others are mostly to the west?"

"Yes," says Amin.

"Well, they are only a couple miles apart, these boys like to be close to each other."

"Yeah, so that they can swap out with each other's wives and daughters," says Terrible with a smile. "True that. But anyway, with the element of surprise, we should be able to hit three to four locations within an hour or so, then meet back here for roll call. Let's start with the grand pooh-bahs," says Malik.

"What about their wives and children?" Amin asks.

"Just the men, anyone else only if they threaten your life," says Malik.

"Malik," says Terrible. "I think that we should kill them all, they have been killing and kidnapping ours without hesitation."

"You're absolutely right, Tee, but we are not them, and we are not going to become them, we answer to a higher self than they do. If we do all the fowl shit they have done, what's the point, there is no difference between us. Now, we are them."

"I get it," says Terrible.

"How do you want the groups broke down?" Amin asks.

"Terrible, Nino, and Pup will go with me. Pasqually, Monk, Cuddy and Ant-Head will go with you."

"Okay, what time are we rolling out?" Amin asks. "As soon as the sun sets."

"Well, let me call everyone in, where are you going to be?"

"Right here, I'm not going anywhere until we are done tonight. And tell Pup to bring six two inch thick ropes," says Malik.

CHAPTER 10

It's almost sunset and all of the team members are busy checking their gear and loading up the vans. Pup is standing there with a puzzled look on his face.

"Malik, what the hell do you want me a to do with these ropes?"

"Give three of them to Amin, we will take the other three. Tell Amin that the leaders of each group at his three locations are to be hung."

Malik opens the door to his van and steps inside, Nino is driving. As soon as Pup piles in they drive off. Thirty minutes later and Malik and his team are pulling up outside the house belonging to their first target, a Klansmen. The house is surrounded by old tires, run-down cars, parts of old refrigerators and stoves. The house itself is a one-story, four-room leaner in disrepair. Malik moves slowly and quietly up to a window on the side of the house and peeps in. He spots the main target sitting in the living room talking to a small group of four to five men. Looking past them, he also sees three women sitting around a table in the kitchen. Malik ducks down and retraces his steps. He then signals to Nino and Pup the number and location of the men and women, then motions for them to go around back. Terrible moves around to the front door as Malik looks and finds a hand sized rock to toss through the window as a diversion.

"On three," says Malik to Terrible then begins the countdown.

"One, two, three!" Malik throws the rock threw the window smashing the glass as Terrible kicks in the front door and Nino and Pup send the back door crashing to the floor!

"Hands up, motherfuckers, don't move!" screams Terrible.

The women scream as Nino and Pup rush over slapping, grabbing and throwing them to the floor.

"Get your stinking asses up and get in there and shut the fuck up!" screams Pup.

The Klansmen and their women are terrified and completely caught off guard. "What the hell is this?" says the Klan leader, a skinny, toothless old drunk that can hardly stand.

"You NIGGERS in a lot of fuckin' trouble, you don't know who the hell your fucking with boy!" he says.

"Yes, we do," says Malik.

"You must be the leader of the group." Malik slaps him in the face with his handgun. The Klansmen falls to the floor, blood gushing from his nose. One of the women, the fat one with the dirty blond hair jumps up and tries to attack Malik, but Terrible round house kicks her in the face. She crumples to the floor unconscious.

"What do you guys want!" asks the Klansmen holding the other women.

"RETRIBUTION, fat boy, RETRIBUTION," says Pup.

"Cover them!" says Malik as he checks the other parts of the house. He finds a small closet just off the kitchen. "You two women get over here now!" yells Malik. The women are hesitant, not knowing what's going to happen. "I said get your asses over here!" Malik cocks the hammer on his .45 and points it at the women. Slowly their fat protector releases them and they make their way over to where Malik is standing with the closet door open, clutching on to each other.

"Go ahead, get in there." Nino lifts the woman that was knocked out up, and pulls her over to the closet, and tosses her inside, then closes the door. Malik takes one of the chairs from the dinner table and props it up under the door knob. The women begin screaming and pleading. "Hey, let us out of here, you fucking assholes, you're going to pay for this!"

"Shut up! One more word, and I'm shooting through this door!" says Nino.

Malik looks over at the leader of the group who is still bleeding badly. "Bring him outside, little bruh," says Malik to Terrible.

"You two know what to do with those four," says Malik.

"Hey, just one minute, we are not bothering you guys," says the Klansmen with the thick reading glasses on, but before he can finish, Nino shoots him square in the head and Pup starts in on the others. Shooting them all, one by one. Terrible marches the Klan leader outside where Malik has found a tree and has tossed one of the ropes over a sturdy branch. He walks over to the Klansmen and tapes his mouth shut, then tapes his hands behind his back. Malik orders him to step up on the chair but he refuses. Terrible hits him upside the head with the butt of his AR 15 assault rifle.

"Get your ass up on that chair or die right here," he says. The Klan leader reluctantly takes the first step up, then the second. Malik slides the noose over his head, moving it down to his neck and pushing the knot up so that it tightens. "This is for all the people's lives you've unmercifully destroyed. The Black, Brown, Red, and the Yellow in the name of protecting your own. People who have never harmed you in any way. This is for your greed and selfishness. And just so you know, all of your kind will be following you to hell soon!" The Klansmen tries to free himself but terrible steps up and kicks the chair from under him. The Klan leader struggles briefly, kicking his feet and jerking before all movement comes to a halt. Nino and Pup run out the house over to where Malik and Terrible are by the tree. "We are finished!" says Pup.

"Let's get out of here!" says Malik.

Two miles away, Amin has three terrified white men lying face down on the floor in their home at gun point. He orders one of them to stand up and get on top of the coffee table in the center of the room. Amin tapes his mouth then his hands behind his back, before tossing one end of the rope over a ceiling beam, pulling it down and placing the noose around the guy's neck. Cuddy walks over and kicks the other two in the ribs, before shooting them both in the head.

"BLACK POWER!" says Cuddy. Amin stands in front of the man on the table.

"This is for my Godchildren," he says before snatching the table from under him and throwing it up against the wall.

Malik is at his second location, no one is there except an old man and his woman, whom Terrible has tied to a chair, and blindfolded. The man is sitting there silently; he knows that his time has come, and that these men will not show him mercy.

"Can I ask why you are doing this?" he asks.

Nino walks over to him and cracks him upside his head. "You know why!" he says.

Monk walks over. "Let me handle this one," he says.

"Get your sorry ass up!" Monk orders. He then snatches the guy up to his feet, taping his mouth, then his hands behind his back, before marching him out to the front porch where he stands him in a chair, puts the rope around his neck and tosses the other end between one of the roofing beans. He then walks back over to the man without saying a word and kicks the chair from under the racist. The old man jerks briefly then dies. "Let's move!" says Terrible.

Amin has come up on a meeting of Klansmen at his second location, inside a large brown barn where bales of cotton are stacked floor to ceiling. "I count ten men," says Amin.

"Me too," says Pasqually.

Amin signals to Ant-Head to check the house. They all wait for him to return, listening and watching the men inside. Moments later Ant-Head is crouching beside Amin. "Two women," says Ant-Head.

Amin pauses, looks around, then turns back to Ant-Head. "Cut the phone lines," he says. Ant-Head disappears around the corner. "We are going to kill them all and burn this barn down. Cuddy get the grenades," says Amin. Cuddy rushes back to the van where monk is keeping a watchful eye on things. "I need the grenades, bruh," says Cuddy.

Monk grabs the small crate holding twelve grenades then hands them to Cuddy who returns back to the barn where Amin, Pasqually, and Ant-Head are keeping a close eye on the men in the barn. They each remove one grenade form the box before taking a position by a window or door on all four sides. One by one, they pull the pin then toss their grenades into the group of men. The first blast taking the occupants totally by surprises. There is screaming, yelling, cries of pain, and pandemonium by the time the second grenade lands inside. Seeing it, the men try to dive for cove, but the third and fourth grenades land exploding blowing them apart. Amin and the others rush in with silencers attached to their weapons looking for any signs of life among the supremacist. Those not already dead are shot. The two women inside the house hear the explosions, peep out, and see a large man dressed in all black clothing, black mask, with an automatic weapon in his hand going inside the barn door, and they both rush into one of the bed rooms to call the police, but they discover that the line is dead. Outside Amin and his team have gotten back into the van and are driving off.

Malik, Pup, Terrible-T, and Nino have arrived back at Amin's place and are busy taking off their gear and storing it. "That guy at the last spot almost gutted me with that hunting knife he had hidden inside his boot!" says Pup.

"You cannot allow your anger to distract you," says Malik.

"Yeah," says Nino, "'Cause when you are distracted, you distract us and put all our lives in danger."

"I know better, I was just tired of hearing that N word."

"Well, you'd better get used to it 'cause there is more to come," Terrible suggests.

"I'm exhausted!" says Nino. Moments later, Amin and the others are heard pulling up in front of the house then getting out the van and walking into the house. Cuddy is very excited. "If you hear any noise, it's just me and the boys!" he sings.

Everyone smiles and breathes a sigh of relief seeing everyone is back and unharmed. They all embrace.

"How did it go?" Malik asks.

"Like clockwork," says Amin.

"Nineteen kills, what about you?"

"Sixteen," says Malik.

"Pup almost bought it."

"What!" say Cuddy, as he, Pasqually, Monk, and Ant-Head begin removing their gear also. "Well, I think we all know the shit is going to hit the fan in the morning!" says Pasqually with a smirk.

"And they are not going to believe whites are behind this," says Ant-Head. "They may link this to the two busters being snatched," suggests Nino. "We just need to be very careful from here on out. Cover your tracks," says Amin.

"Even though we wore masks, I'm sure the women at those spots recognized out voices as being black. This is why I asked that we be allowed to kill everyone," says Terrible. "We have already covered that, so let's move on to other possibilities. We have eight objectives in this area to cover. So let's map out our strike on them," says Malik.

"I say we handle things the same way we did tonight," Pasqually suggests.

"Me too," says Monk.

"Okay then," says Malik.

"All we need now is a timeline."

"Big bruh, I think we should base the time line on what type of response we get from the police," says Amin.

"Good idea, Malik, you know you'll be watched," says Cuddy.

"I know, so let's plan the next strike for this someday next month. That way we will have time to see what's out there and plan for it."

"These pecker heads will spread the word among themselves and tighten up their security, and be prepared for us next time," Amin suggests.

Malik stands there briefly in thought before snapping out of it and heading for the front door. "I'll see you guys in thirty days," he says.

It's late. Aunt Pat is awakened from her sleep as Malik makes his way into his front door. She fell asleep on the couch waiting on his return home.

"Malik, is that you, honey?" she asks.

"Yes, it's me, Aunt Pat," says Malik.

"What are you doing here?"

"I wanted to speak with you, but I cannot seem to catch you lately."

"Yeah, I've been kinda busy." Malik takes his coat off then hangs it up inside the hallway closet, before walking into the living room where Aunt Pat is curled up on the couch.

"Come sit here beside me," she says.

Malik walks over and takes a seat. "You know I remember when you were a little boy, you were always so protective of the family and I can tell when you are in that mind frame."

"I'm okay, Auntie."

"I know that, I just want you to know I'm here for you. That you are not alone in this family."

"I know that."

"Jada is worried to death about you. She has been having bad dreams."

Malik smiles. "That girl and her dreams. INSHALLAH. I'll call her tomorrow."

"Make sure you do before she drives me crazy." Aunt Pat and Malik both laugh. Aunt Pat stands and opens her arms to Malik. "Now give me a hug so I can go home," she says. Malik stands and hugs her tightly. "It's late, you sure you don't want to sleep in the guest room?" Malik asks.

"Honey, I have so much work to do around the house tomorrow. I've got to go, but I'll call you, I love you."

"I love you too, Auntie." Aunt Pat slides on her brown suede jacket, blows Malik a kiss, then walks out the door. Malik turns and heads upstairs to his bedroom and peeps inside, Sakinah is in bed. He heads to the bathroom, undresses, then steps into the shower, allowing the water to run directly over his face and head. A short while later, Malik steps out and walks into his bedroom where he slips on his pajama bottoms, then slides under the covers and up next to Sakinah, who has her back to him, lying motionless with her eyes wide open.

It's early the next morning and Sakinah is up preparing breakfast. As she is doing so, a special news report flashes across the screen as three reporters are broadcasting live from three different locations, the death of members of white supremacist groups. Sakinah rushes upstairs to inform Malik of the newscast, but when she arrives, she finds him still in bed sound asleep. She stands there silently in the door way staring at her husband.

Ms. Norma is sitting in her living room sipping green tea when the news report is broadcast. She gets up, walks over, and turns the television off. She then gets down or both of her knees, cupping her hands together, then looking toward the sky. "Please, God, protect my baby, please! Please!"

Across town, Jada is watching the broadcast also and yelling for her mom to come and see it. Aunt Pat rushes into the room as the bodies are being removed from the barn. "Your nephew done that!" says Jada.

"Don't say that!" yells Aunt Pat. "Don't you ever say those words aloud again, nor to anyone else, do you understand?" asks Aunt Pat.

"Yes Mom, but I told you Malik was not going to take his children being killed lying down."

"You don't know who done this, so try to remember to act like you don't."

Captain Twyman has arrived at the scene of the grenade blasts inside the barn with Taylor, Brooks, and a host of other officers, detectives, and forensic specialist who are going over the crime scene and talking with the two women.

"Ma'am, did you see anyone?" Brooks asks.

"NO!" says the large, blue-eyed blond woman. "We just heard the blasts, the yelling and then it was quiet," she says. "We were afraid to come outside, we tried to call the police, but the phone was dead," says her girlfriend, the short, petite, chainsmoker.

Captain Twyman stands there listening and looking over the scene. "Okay, ladies, I need you to go with one of my officers so that we can get a formal statement."

Before he can arrange this another officer walks up. "Chief, we've found grenade fragments and ten bodies," he says.

"Damn! What the hell is going on here?" the captain asks.

Just then another officer walks up with the radio. "Chief, we've got bodies at five more locations and at least five of the dead were lynched."

"Were there any witnesses?" Detective Taylor asks.

"There are reports of some women being locked in a closet at one scene, and others tied up at four of the other locations."

"So whomever done this wanted to kill only the men?" says Brooks to no one in particular.

"Looks that way," says the captain.

"Not just the men, but all white men and known members of white power groups," says Taylor.

"So do we have a war on our hands between the different groups?" Twyman asks.

"That's possible," says Taylor.

"Some of these Neo groups view the Klan and the Aryans as weak and lukewarm to their cause."

"Or maybe we have a group of people victimized by these groups who have decided to victimize them?" Brooks suggests.

The captain turns to him. "Blacks?" he asks.

"Could be, stranger things have happened," says Brooks.

FBI Agents Branch and Oliver are arriving at the crime scene where the women were locked inside the closet. They flash their badges and proceed into the house where the women are sitting at the kitchen table. They clear permission with the officers in charge to speak with them.

"Ladies, I'm FBI Agent Oliver and this is Agent Branch. We would like to ask you a couple questions, we know that this is a difficult time for you that you are tired, it's been hell of a night for you. But did any of you see these men faces?"

"No, they all had on masks," says the tallest of the three women.

"Okay, do any of you have any idea why these men came here and done this?" Oliver asks.

"No, they just ran in there screaming and pushing us around. By the way, my name is Alice, and one of those bastards kicked me and knocked me out, then threw me in the closet!"

"I'm sorry to hear that, are you okay?"

"Hell, yeah, it'll take a lot more than that to put me down."

"Okay, Alice, so you heard their voices, they spoke?" Agent Branch asks.

"Yes, they didn't say much after they had us all doing what they wanted."

"What did they sound like? Did their voices sound like they were from around here?"

"Yeah, but the one guy who slapped me sounded like he was black."

Branch and Oliver glance at each other before Branch continues questioning Alice.

"Can you recall his physical description? Was he tall, short, fat, slim, heavy, what?"

"He was medium height slim built, I think it was hard to tell, they all had on these vest and baggy blacks pants."

"Okay, Alice, you are doing fine, is there anything else you can remember about these men that sticks out?"

"One of my friends asked them why they were doing this, and one of them said retribution."

"Thank you, all of you, we many need to contact you again later if we get a suspect, to see if either of you can recognize his voice."

Captain Twyman, Detectives Taylor, Brooks, and a wide spectrum of local law enforcement are now at the scene of Malik's second stop last night and are going over the notes and facts related to all six locations. "Okay, we've got six murder scenes, with twenty-five bodies," says Twyman.

"That's correct," says Taylor.

"But I don't understand something here. You see we have four groups of women, two groups seem to confirm the size and height of the attackers and their methods as the same. While the other two groups differ in their description of the attackers, but the method is the same for all?"

They all stand there lost in thought momentarily. "There were two groups!" says Brooks excitedly.

"There had to be," he says. One of the crime scene investigators looks up from his notes. "None of the witnesses seen what took place outside, but I'm certain that these men had someone covering their backs while they were inside. I'm going to have my people widen their search of the property," he says.

"That makes sense. So what we are looking for then is an assault team, possibly special forces or people with military training," the captain asks.

"We can start with the local recruiters and see who is in the area. I'm sure Agents Oliver and Branch can help us on this," says Taylor.

"Military records are federal and unless we have a suspect, they are off limits," says the scene investigator.

"We may be able to get some assistance with that," says the captain. "Brooks, I want a team to seal off the area around each crime scene for one hundred meters in each direction, then comb over every inch of it looking for anything the suspects may have dropped. A cigarette butt, a candy wrapper, soft drink can, anything!"

"Okay, I'll handle this myself chief, and meet all of you back at the station later." Brooks walks back up to the house. "I want all investigators and reports in the situation room tonight at eight sharp!" says Twyman.

Malik has finally awakened after sleeping soundly all morning. He heads downstairs and into the kitchen where he looks and sees Sakinah sitting out by the pool. He stops at the refrigerator and removes a small bottle of orange juice before heading out to the patio where Sakinah is. He leans over and gives her a kiss.

"Good afternoon," he says before taking the seat next to her.

"You slept all morning," Sakinah says.

"I see, I was tired."

"From the news broadcast that's been playing all morning I see why," says Sakinah matter of factly.

"Oh yeah, what did they report?"

"That twenty-five known white male supremacist where killed last night, in six different locations in Mobile, and that six of them were lynched, one at each location."

"Anything else."

"That's all," says Sakinah.

"Oh, Aunt Pat called, she says that she needs to see you at the office tomorrow morning God willing, regarding the Mahogany account." Malik smiles at his wife, and her ability to be pleasant under the circumstances.

"Let's go on a picnic right now," he suggested.

"What!" says Sakinah, taken completely by surprise.

"Let's do it. Let's pack a picnic basket and go out to the lake." Malik gives her a broad smile. "Are you serious?"

"Yes, come on." Malik reaches out his hand for his wife and she takes it. "Put on one of those sexy summer dresses and I'll put us something together in the basket."

"Okay, give me a second."

"Sakinah bounces up the stairs, smiling as Malik walks into the kitchen and begins removing food from the fridge and the pantry and placing it inside a brown wicker basket. Moments later, Sakinah skips down the stairs to the front door, where she finds Malik waiting with the basket in his hand. "I'm ready."

"Yes you are sexy, let's go."

FBI Agents Branch and Oliver are driving down the highway trying to digest all the information they have collected all day from the different crimes scenes. Agent Oliver cannot shake the feeling that Malik is somehow involved, based on the descriptions all the women gave. He looks over to Branch, who has a phone unit plugged into the dashboard. "I'm getting no answer at the Davenport home," says Branch.

"Try the law firm then, I want to know where Mr. Davenport was last night," says Oliver.

Miles away, Malik and Sakinah are holding hands walking through Liberty Park looking for a quiet spot by the lake to put their blanket down. They find one and unfold the quilt his grandmother Ruth stitched together, then take a seat.

"It's so beautiful out here today, look at all the ducks and swans," says Sakinah.

"Yes, they are beautiful, and so are you," says Malik, Sakinah is beaming.

"Now you come here beautiful." Malik reaches over and pulls Sakinah on top of him and kisses her passionately. Seconds later, Sakinah pulls back, then looks her husband in his eyes. "Wow, I see you haven't lost your touch."

Sakinah smiles, tracing one finger over and around Malik's lips. "I hope that is always the case with you and I," he says.

"I don't see why it wouldn't be?"

"Well, things have suddenly changed. A lot."

"But not between you and me, Malik."

"There are things that could affect us both going on right now. This killing, I don't like it, at all."

Sakinah cuts him off placing a finger over his lips. "I didn't like it when you went to Vietnam, I waited, worried, prayed a lot. A lot! But you said you had to go, and so I accepted that. You are not a bad person Malik, I know this. I know you, I check you out all the time. People who know you, absolutely love you, you have a good heart. I've done nothing but thought about what's going on. I don't like it either, but only because I could lose you. But make no mistake about it, I understand. I know something has to be done about it. Fighting oppression in any form, whether it's an oppressive government or a group of Hillbillies, means possible loss of life for the good guys. I've watched our people die because of these people and mostly up until now the dying has all been one-sided. So I'm going to stand by my man, the love of my life, just like the racist white girls stand by theirs after their boys have returned from murdering some of us for the fun of it."

Malik takes her face in his hands, looking deep into her eyes. "You do realize that things are going to get worse?" he asks.

"I ain't going nowhere baby and that includes crazy." Sakinah smiles. "These people murdered our children." Tears form at the corners of Sakinah's eyes. Malik kisses them away then hugs Sakinah tightly as she lays her head on his chest. "I know baby, I know."

Downtown Mobile, a group of white men are standing around a newspaper stand, that has a shoe polishing stand next to it. An elderly black man is polishing two of the men's shoes in silence, as they discuss the killings in the newspapers. "I can't believe this, twenty five white men dead, six of 'em lynched, it just don't sit right with me," says the man with the black slip on loafers.

"Me neither," says his old friend Barry, who just happened by the newsstand, and decided to get a little polish put on his shoes also. "Their saying there is bad blood between these people, but I think that's crap! I'm telling you, it's some of those militant niggers on the loose," says Barry.

"They don't have none of them down here, those kinda boys are all up north. Niggers down here know their place," says the man in the black loafers.

"They use to until they went and allowed them to vote and hold public office. Now everything done gone to hell," says Barry.

"You're right, they're not afraid anymore. They'll talk back and some of em' will stare you right in the eye."

"Whatever is going on I'll sleep a lot better when they catch 'em," says Barry.

"Me too, but until they do, I'm keeping my twelve gauge right by the bedroom door."

"You'd better," says Barry.

"They lynched six white man, now that's a first," he says. The old shoe shiner interrupts them.

"I'm done, sir," he says.

"Thanks boy," says Barry. Who pays for both of the shines, then he and his friend get up folding their papers under their arms, before heading down the street. The shoe shiner watches the two of them then smiles to himself. "Thus said the Lord, as you sow, so shall you reap, amen," he says before he begins packing up his brushes and polish.

At the FBI Headquarters, Agents Branch, Oliver, Chief Jacocks, and several other agents and staff are sitting in a conference room with charts, graphs and photos of the six murder scenes. "We may have here a case of reverse racism as Agent Oliver has suggested," says Chief Jacocks.

"Or what one of the witnesses overheard described as RETRIBUTION," he says.

"Chief, maybe we should begin by trying to nail down what link all of these people had. I mean whoever done this appears to have known exactly who they were looking for and where to look. I don't believe that their racial beliefs are the link," says Oliver.

"Why, because of the lynchings?" the chief asks.

"Exactly!"

"Maybe their racial bigotry is the link but not the method for selection?" suggests one of the junior agents.

"From the information we were able to gather at the scene, it appears that all the men that were lynched held leadership positions within the group," says Branch.

"So the leadership is being singled out?" asks Chief Jacocks.

"Held responsible for spreading the hate and violence," Branch suggests.

"Though everyone dies," he adds.

"Except the women," Oliver says.

"Man, we may have to protect this people," says the chief.

"They may not want our protection, Chief, most of them have their own security," says the junior agent.

"Good!" shouts Agent Branch.

"What's that supposed to mean?" the chief snaps at Branch.

"Nothing," he says. "You do understand that no matter how much hate these people bring to the world, if they are being targeted we have an obligation to protect them."

"I know, it's just that these white power characters have done this very thing to so many people and now we have to protect them?"

Agent Branch clearly doesn't like the idea of this, "That's your job," says the chief. "They deserve this, they created it, it was just a matter of time before someone out there got tired of them killing innocent people for fun. These people don't have any understanding."

"That's not for you to decide!" says Chief Jacocks.

"Who decided that couple in Fayetteville North Carolina had to die?" asks Branch.

"What couple?"

"The couple that was murdered recently by those Aryan Army Soldier at Fort Bragg. They were out walking, holding hands, in love, when a group of these clowns drove up and shot them both in the head. They both died. Eight months later the same thing happened in Denver, where does it end? When a group of people don't see you as human, you are nothing but target practice," says Branch.

"I hear you, but this is not the way."

"I'm not so sure, Chief."

"Gentlemen!" Oliver stands up between the chief and his partner. "We are all friends here and on the same team, let's not go after each other, this is a touchy issue for all of us," he says.

The chief and Branch make eye contact signaling a truce. "Okay, let's begin by doing background checks on all ex-service men in the area."

"Chief the one witness said one of the men sounded Black!" says one of the female agents as she pores over her notes.

"I know, but perhaps he wanted to give that impression?" says the chief.

"Or maybe he was a hip white boy you know that there are a lot of them walking around today. If you did not see them in person, you'd have absolutely no idea that the person you were speaking to was white. They call them wiggers," says Branch, who stands and gather his things before leaving the room. The chief watches him leave, angry over the disrespect.

"I got him, Chief, he will be all right," says Oliver.

"He'd better be!" says the chief. Oliver runs over catching Agent Branch at the elevators. The doors open and they both step inside. Branch presses the button labeled "Garage."

"You cool?" Oliver asks.

"Yeah, I'm cool, what's next?"

"Let's see if Mr. Davenport is home yet."

Malik and Sakinah are holding hands as they walk up to the door of their home and walk inside. "I'll check the answering machine," says Sakinah.

"Okay, I'll put these things away. Hey, let's take a quick shower together and fix dinner, like we used to do, just the two of us. No phone, no answering the door, nothing, just us?" suggests Malik.

"You'd better put your car in the garage then and turn on the porch light," says Sakinah.

"Good idea baby." Malik puts the basket on the chair, then goes outside to move his car. After doing so, he heads back to the house just as Agents Branch and Oliver are pulling into his driveway. They both exit their car, then walked over to Malik, before he gets to his door.

"Mr. Davenport, I was wondering if we could have a moment of your time," Oliver asks. "Sure." Malik back tracks, stepping back into the driveway.

"What can I do for you?" he asks. "Have you heard about the murders and lynching that took place the other night?" ask Oliver.

"I did."

"Well, can you tell us where you were Sunday night?"

"What time Sunday night?"

"Around 9:00 p.m."

"I was home," says Malik.

"Where you alone?" asks Oliver.

"No, I was with my wife."

"Is she home now?"

"Yes, she is. Is there a problem? Would you like to speak to her?"

"That's not necessary right now. One other question, did you hear that the two suspects in the murder of your children were taken away from the sheriff deputies?"

"I did."

"Do you have any idea who might have done that Mr. Davenport?"

"Not one, but I'm hoping you guys are doing a lot better job than I am."

"Oh, you can count on it, Mr. Davenport, for sure." Oliver gives him the once-over look.

"I'm glad to hear it, now if you two have nothing further, I'd like to go and prepare dinner for my wife."

"No problem, but we may need to speak with you again as the case develops."

"I'll be right here. I'm not going anywhere until the murderers of my son and daughter have paid for the lives they took."

With that said, Malik turns and walks back into his home, closing the door behind him. Agents Oliver and Branch return to their car and back out the driveway. Oliver is driving. "Something tells me that he knows a lot more than he is saying," Oliver suggests.

"That doesn't mean he is involved," says Branch. "I think that we should do a background check on Mr. Davenport. Let's find out exactly what type of Military training he has."

"I'm hungry and tired," says Branch.

"Drop me off at home," he says.

As Malik enters his home and closes the door, he finds Sakinah standing behind it. "What did they want?" she asks.

"To know where I was Sunday night."

"What did you tell them?"

"That I was home with you."

"I have the shower running," she says.

"Let's not keep it waiting." Malik takes her hand and leads the way to their bedroom where they undress each other before walking into the shower. Forty-five minutes later, they are downstairs dressed for dinner with candles burning and smooth jazz playing in the background. Malik is wearing a dark blue linen shirt with matching dark blue linen slacks, blue calf skin shoes, no socks.

Sakinah is wearing a dark blue spaghetti strap summer dress, blue linen heels, and her mother's white pearl earrings and matching necklace. Tonight, they are having a simple chef salad with fresh salmon with lemon juice, garlic, tomatoes, fresh red onions and peppers. Malik takes her plate from the countertop then places it in front of her before taking his seat.

"Thank you," says Sakinah.

"You're welcome. You know baby, you are really kinda cute," says Malik as he sits back in his chair and takes a good look at Sakinah, the candle light dancing off her almond-shaped eyes."

"What you do mean kinda?" she asks with playful frown.

"Like kinda!" They both laugh and nibble at their food. "You are kinda handsome, now that I've taken a good look at you under candle light."

"What do you mean kinda, I'm fine!" The two of them laugh even harder, then Sakinah is distracted by a song on the stereo.

"Turn that up baby, that's my song," she says. Malik moves over to the mini stereo and increases the volume.

"Know that I'm living for the love of you, all that I'm giving is for the love of you," sings Sakinah.

"The Isley Bothers, I love that song, no one does it better," she says. "Would you like to dance, my queen?"

"Yes, my king." Malik turns the music up before taking Sakinah's hand and leading her in a slow dance as she continues to sing along.

It's one month later to the day that Malik and Faze Two first dealt a blow to White Power in Mobile, Alabama, and Malik is at the location of his first target. A church. Inside is a congregation of supremacist listening to a hate speech. Outside is six heavily armed guards. Malik and his team are wearing Military night vision goggles. Their carrying C-4 explosives, grenades and AR 15 asasult rifles with silencers.

"Terrible we are going to place C-4 around the entire church and blow the whole thing," says Malik.

"I have enough to blow twenty churches bruh."

"Good, but first we need to take out the sentries."

"I count six of them with automatic weapons," says Pup.

"Yeah, four out front and two in the back," says Nino.

"Tee, can you handle the two out back?" Malik asks.

"No problem." Terrible moves out, making sure to stay behind the tree line as he makes a wide arc to the rear of the church.

"We don't want them giving an alarm, so we need to separate them," Malik suggests.

"Nino, you move to the left, Pup, you go right. Toss a couple stones or something to get them to move apart to the left and right, and I'll hit them from behind," says Malik.

Once in place, Pup tosses a couple stones just to the left of the guard standing on the front left corner of the church, he walks over to take a look and one of his partners moves over slightly behind him to cover him. At that very moment, Nino does the same thing on the right side and the guard on that corner moves over peeping out into the dark to see the origin of the sound, Malik takes advantage of the separation and shoots the two guards to the left in the back of their heads. Pup rushes up out of the tree line and he and Malik kill the other two moving in on Nino. Seconds later, Terrible rejoins them after having finished off the two guards in back. "All clear out back," he says.

"Let's place the C-4," says Malik. Terrible removes the duffle bag from off his shoulders, and they all join in separating it, setting the detonators and timers, then they all move to one side of the church and place the C-4 in a spot that will provide the best affect. Once done, Malik peeps inside one of the back windows as the preacher is delivering his sermon. "I'm telling you, if we don't stand up and unite against the Jew and Niggers, they are going to take over the world! Them damn Jews are buying up every damn square inch of our country. This is our land, our forefathers worked hard to settle this country, under attack almost every day from injen savages, and I'll be damned if I'll sit back and watch these Coons take it from us without a fight!"

The crowd roars with a thunderous applause. The preacher waits for it to die down then continues.

"I'm telling all of ya, that this is war!"

Again, there is a loud applause, as Malik turns back away from the window. "You've got that right," he says.

He then moves away, back to where he and the rest of the team can watch the explosion from a safe distance. Once there, he activates the detonator and looks at his team. "HEIL, HITLER!" he says. They all repeat the twisted salute, then Malik presses the button. *Boom*, sixty men dead.

"Let's move," he says.

Amin and his team are crouched down outside an old house in need of drastic repair. Inside a middle-aged white couple are engaged in having sex. Outside the team is clearly frustrated. "Shall we wait until they are done?" asks Pasqually.

"Let's burn it down!" says Cuddy.

"Malik said no women or children," says Amin.

"They have raped and killed our women and children. What you think that was an accident?" Cuddy asks.

"You think I don't know this?" Amin asks.

"Well, act like you do, Malik ain't here!"

"Yes, he is!" says Amin.

"Well, tell him this one is on me, it's for all the black women who were pregnant and yet these people beat them, raped them and cut their stomachs open. Ripping their fetus out and stumping them to death or smashing them with their rifle butt." Cuddy returns back to the van, retrieving a two gallon can of gasoline. He splashes it all over the front and sides of the house before taking out a book of matches, striking one, then throwing it down into the gas. Instantly there is a "WOSH."

The house is instantly in engulfed. Cuddy walks around to the bedroom window breaks the glass, yells "AMISTAD," before emptying his nine-millimeter Barretta into the couple. He then walks past Amin and the other team member before stopping.

"Y'all coming?" he asks before heading back to the van and getting in on the passenger side and closing the door. Amin and the others watch him momentarily before running to the van themselves, and driving off.

Malik and his team are inside the home of Klan Wizard Mark Bowers. They have him sitting in a chair in the living room, he is alone. "Are you Mark Bowers?" Malik asks.

"Yes, I am."

"Are you the Imperial Wizard of the KKK?"

"Yes I am, what is it you Niggers want?"

"We want you to say your prayers," says Nino.

"You Niggers aint got the nerve, so why don't you all just go on and get the hell out my house!" Bowers yells.

Monk comes over with his pistol drawn and points it right between Bower's eyes.

"Say your good night, and just before I rock you, I want you to know that Jesus was a Black man, just like his mother." Monk pulls the trigger blowing the back of Mark Bowers head off. He slumps over in the chair.

"Burn it!" says Malik.

An hour later, Malik and his team are pulling up at Amin's, only to find that Amin and the others have already made it back. He and the others walk inside and embrace everyone, happy that once again none of them were hurt or injured in anyway.

"How many kills?" Malik asks.

"Twelve," says Amin. "What about you?"

"About seventy, we walked up on a church rally," says Malik.

"Damn!" The National Guard will be called in once this gets out," says Ant-Head.

"They'll probably set up a task force," Amin suggests.

"Yeah, we should lay low for a little longer this time," says Pasqually. "Well, tonight finished up the known Hate groups in this small area anyway. I've been going over the information that Hugh Lamont gave us and it IDs the leadership across the country. I think if we cut off the heads, the bodies will die," says Malik.

"I see where you're coming from on this," says Nino. "It's exactly the plan they have lived by where we are concerned, 'cause all of our strong leaders to date with potential to really get this Nation together were murdered."

"If we go after the leaders we can afford to wait until they are isolated and then make the kill," suggests Malik.

"That way, we don't put everyone at risk."

"Okay, how do we isolate them?" Pup asks.

"We select the target, shadow him and pick the best opportunity to terminate him," says Malik.

"I like that," says Amin.

"Me too," says Cuddy.

"Uh, Cuddy, don't you have something to tell the brother?" Amin asks.

Cuddy rolls his eyes at Amin. "Yeah, well, I smoked the Aryan target and his girlfriend."

"I clearly asked everyone not to kill women and children."

"I know but they were in there fucking and drinking. What was I supposed to do, wait until he came? Hell, they can't fuck anyway, the shit could have taken hours and we didn't have time to be hiding in the shadows until he was done. These clowns procreate their seed while destroying ours. That's just one less vehicle to bring that shit in the world through."

Malik and the others stand there; Cuddy is very upset about the standing order. "This is not about emotions little brother, this some ugly shit we are dealing with and I know it's hard not to go mad with thoughts of everything we have lived through with these people, but we have got to stay cool, or we lose everything," says Malik. "That's right, I'm not trying to get caught up in this shit, I'm not afraid to die, either. But if we can win without casualties, why not do so?" asks Nino.

"That's exactly my meaning," says Malik.

"So what's next?" Amin asks.

"David Shook, he's a Grand Dragon in Macon Georgia,"

"When?" asks Pasqually.

"As soon as you spot him and terminate him. Your time line is your own. Next is him!" Malik points to a recent photo of the next target. "Robert Whitney, he's in Jacksonville North Carolina. Nino, he's all yours. Next is this buster, David Remy, he's in Little Rock, Arkansas. Cuddy, he's yours," says Malik.

"No problem," says Cuddy.

"There's going to be a major fall out once the shit hit's the fan, and we may not see each other for a while. I'll send the assignments by one of sweet Scoots people or by Hasheem. I've got to get home, Shukran, I love all of you."

Sakinah is watching the news special report when Malik walks into the bedroom, giving her a quick kiss, undressing, then heading to the shower. "They are reporting that seventy people died in an explosion south of here in a Church and six other bodies appear to have been shot at the scene. They've found two charred bodies in some half burned house out by Mitchlin Lake. They were shot also.

Another reporter is now at some location where three white men were lynched and their home burned to the ground. No report yet of whether or not bodies where inside. The reporter says that there are more reports coming in," says Sakinah.

"I'm going to take a quick shower honey, ten minutes, I'll be right out. Has anyone called?"

"Just your mother." Malik steps into the shower, allowing the cool water to run over his entire body before lathering up, rinsing off a final time. He steps out then walks into his bedroom drying off. "We are going to switch things up a bit, I won't be going anywhere for a while."

"This is causing National attention," says Sakinah.

"We knew that it would, the attention is necessary to bring the changes we are hoping for," Malik suggests.

"Call your mother, she's worried and waiting on your call. She's not going to sleep until she hears from you." Malik walks over to his side of the bed, picks up the phone and dials his mother's number. She picks up on the first ring.

"Hi, Mom. Yes, I'm fine. I know, but don't worry. Hey, why don't you, Aunt Pat and Jada come over for dinner tomorrow INSHAALLAH. Six o'clock sharp. I love you too. Good night, Mother." Malik hangs up the phone then slides in underneath the covers. Sakinah grabs Malik, pulling him to her. She then kisses him several times all over his face. "Boy, you are crazy!" she says playfully, Malik smiles.

"Crazy, crazy, crazy!" says Sakinah. She then climbs on top of Malik and once again she smothers him with kisses.

It's early the next morning; the sun is rising on what looks to be a pleasant sunny day in Mobile. Captain Twyman is in his situation room about to introduce Agent Oliver and Branch to everyone in the room. "We believe that there is a paramilitary group behind these murders. One who has decided to go after hate groups and their leaders. As a result the Justice Department has stepped in and we are forming a joint task force with the federal authorities. These are

Agents John Branch and Clayton Oliver; they will be acting as our liaison with the Feds." Agent Oliver stands.

"At this point we have no leads, whoever these people are, they leave nothing behind, no finger prints, nothing. We have forensic teams going over all eight crime scenes as we speak. And we are checking our files for known Merc's in this area."

"Is it possible that these people may not be from this area?" Brooks asks.

"Yes, it is. And it may be the reason why they decide to hit as many target's as they do in one night."

"Or maybe killing one hundred people in one night keeps them from having to come out so often," Taylor suggests.

"Mr. Oliver, I'm undercover Agent Scooter Bonner." (IT'S SWEET SCOOT.)

"Do you have a motive for these killings, outside of the race card, and if so, why now," he asks. "We believe that the spree of killings may have been sparked by the murder of the Davenport children."

"Okay, but the killings did not start until after the suspects of those murders were hijacked to freedom," says Sweet Scoot.

"We don't know if they went to freedom or death, they simply disappeared. The same group responsible for these murders, may have taken those two, we don't know," says Oliver. "It would fit the pattern," says Branch.

"The people responsible for these killings appear to avoid killing women. They may have felt that the deputies had nothing to do with those two they took, so they spared their lives."

"So they have no interest in killing innocent people?" Brooks asks.

"That appears to be the case. There may be a moral issue against killing women, period," says Branch. Just then, an officer walks in and hands Captain Twyman a report. Which he studies for a moment. "That may have just changed. This report indicates that one of the victims in the fire out on Windel Road was female, and she was shot several times."

"Has anyone spoken to Mr. Davenport?" Brooks asks.

"John and I spoke with him after the first rash of murders, he has an alibi," says Oliver.

"Where was he?"

"Home with his wife."

"That's not an alibi, that's a convenience," says Brooks.

"And why is that detective?" Branch asks.

"Because that's his wife she'll say anything."

"Are you married?" asks Branch.

"NO!" says Brooks.

"I didn't think so."

"Boys! Let's not lose focus. I want a tail put on Mr. Davenport," says Captain Twyman.

"What about a phone tap?" Brooks asks.

"We don't have anything to warrant a tap," the captain says.

"Perhaps tailing him will give us a reason?" suggests Oliver.

"Well, for now, it's all we've got to go on and I must say I'm not too optimistic about this, but you never know," says Twyman. "These recent killings happened almost a month to the day of the last ones. Maybe there is a pattern here?" says Oliver. "Then we need to come up with some type of plan based on that time line," says the captain.

Malik is sitting at his dinner table enjoying a meal with his mother, Aunt Pat, Jada and Sakinah. "Jada, what have you been doing with yourself, you look so pretty," says Ms. Norma.

"Thank you, I'm just running and working out every day."

"Do you have a boyfriend?"

"No, ma'am, not yet."

"She'll only talk him to death," says Malik playfully, Jada sticks her tongue out at him.

"Oh, shut up, Malik."

"That's why that one guy, what was his name, Osman, that's why he stopped calling."

"No, it's not, he wanted me to give him some, and I said no, not until I'm married." Sakinah and Malik burst out laughing; Aunt Pat looks at Jada with surprise. "That's right baby, there is nothing wrong with that," says Ms. Norma. Sakinah is still laughing. "Mom, that girl ain't hardly no virgin!" she says.

"Yes I am!" says Jada.

"Yeah, in that case, so am I," says Malik, smiling. "Please, don't ya'll get her started," says aunt Pat.

"Auntie, you know Jada is always trying to run that 'I'm a virgin' act on Momma."

"Yall just leave her alone," says Ms. Norma.

Again, Jada sticks her tongue out at Malik. "Malik, honey, are you sure that you're ready to come back to work?" Auntie Pat asks.

"Yes, I think it will do me some good." Everyone stops what they are doing and looks at him.

"What!?" says Malik after seeing their expression.

"You know what, you've got a big head, I don't know what it is Sakinah sees in you," says Jada, as she uses both her hands to show Malik's head size.

"Don't talk about my babies' head, it's not big," says Sakinah. She leans over and kisses Malik on the cheek.

"I got my mom's head, so now, what are you saying?" They all look at Ms. Norma and laugh. Just then the phone rings and Malik picks it up.

"Hello, my brother, how are you? Oh yeah, cool, you stay up."

"Who was that?" Sakinah asks.

"Sweet Scoot, he told me to say hello."

Everyone turns back to eating their meal when suddenly the doorbell rings. Malik goes and opens the door, it's Hugh Lamont.

"What's up? Come in," says Malik.

"I need to talk with you, who's here?" Hugh asks.

"My mom, Aunt Pat and Jada, come in and say hello first."

The two of them walk into the dining room where Hugh greets everyone with a kiss and hello.

"Hugh Lamont, come on sit down, and eat something honey," says Mr. Norma.

"I can't, I'm kinda in a hurry, I just need to speak with Malik for a moment."

"Come on," says Malik before leading Hugh Lamont toward his study. They walk in and Malik closes the door. "What's up?" he asks.

"What's up, are you crazy! They say a hundred people were killed the other night!" Hugh Lamont can barely control himself.

"And?"

"And! And! Don't you see that this shit is all the way wrong, you can't just take the law into your own hands."

"Well, tell me something, when these people decided to kill blacks because they did not want them to vote, whose hands was the law in then? When they decided to murder Black men for looking or speaking to white women whose hands was the law in then? When they decided to fire bomb Black Churches, who's hands was the law in then? Are you blind Hugh or just stupid? The irony is that all you knee-grows who obtain what you call success, a home, a bank account, possibly you own business, you all think like that. Suddenly all the shit that's been done to us no longer matters. You don't want to lose nothing, fight for nothing, die for nothing. You are so blinded by the shit you've become, that you can't see that you're already dead or dying. You have no feeling outside of yourself, no sense of touch, just like the car you drive everything you are is for show. But in here!"

Malik points to Hugh Lamont's chest. "You are hollow."

"You're wrong," says Hugh Lamont.

"Am I, I don't think so, you and your kind are enemies of our race. You straddle the fence because your skin color allows you to walk among us, but you hate yourself because of your color, and you're yet to realize that the person responsible for your hatred of yourself is the very person you've become. You may as well join the Klan. Now if you would excuse me, my dinner is getting cold, let yourself out." Malik walks out of the room and back into the dining room leaving Hugh standing there looking dumb founded on what to do or say.

"Where is Hugh?" Sakinah asks.

"He had important business to attend to." Sakinah looks at Malik sensing there is more to the story.

It's around 9:00 a.m. the next morning and Malik has entered his office building. One of the receptionist notices him. "Well, good morning, Mr. Davenport, it's good to see you back with us."

"It's good to be back, Janice, how have you been?"

"I'm fine, my only problem is trying to maintain this diet," says Janice with a frown.

"You're looking as good as ever. I can't believe you have difficulty with your beauty." Malik smiles.

"You are too kind."

"Do I have any old messages?"

"A ton, most of them are already in your office and here are the rest?"

"Thank you," says Malik, before walking to his office, closing the door and plopping down in his chair. He pauses momentarily to reflect on work, the comfort of his chair, and the many photos of his wife and children, before pushing the button on his phone.

"Kim, do you have the Mahogany file. Is she in? Okay, thank you." Malik gets up from his desk, goes out the door and down to his aunt Pat's office where he knocks on her door before entering.

"Well, good morning, aren't you looking handsome!" says Aunt Pat.

"Thank you."

"Are you sure that you are ready to get started with all of this so soon?"

"Yes, I'm sure."

"As you wish."

"I was wondering if I could get a look at the Mahogany file?"

"Sure, I have it right here." Aunt Pat reaches into her desk drawer, removes the file and hands it to her nephew.

"Thanks. When is the case scheduled for prelim?"

"Friday."

"Do you know who the sitting Judge is?"

"C. W. Bey."

"He's a fair judge," says Malik.

"Yes, he has a reputation for listening to both sides."

"I'd like to argue this case."

"Do you think you can be ready?"

"I do."

"Well, it's yours."

"Thank you, Auntie." Malik turns to leave then stops.

"Can I take you to lunch?"

"I'd like that." Malik walks back to his office, closes the door and places the file he was just given in the center of his desk. Retaking his seat, he calls Kim a second time and instructs her to hold all of his calls.

Detectives Taylor and Brooks are stepping out into the afternoon sunshine for the first time as they prepare to leave the station. Brooks tosses Taylor the car keys, they get in and Taylor pulls out the parking lot.

"I don't think mobilizing a bunch of undercover units this time next month is going to solve a thing," he says.

"It will if Davenport is responsible for this and he leads us to the rest of the guys," says Brooks.

"That's just it, what if it's not him. Or what if he doesn't move with the people doing the murders?"

"Then we are stuck like chuck, because we have no other leads to go on."

"If the people responsible for this are black, do you think other blacks seeing the results will go to the police?" asks Taylor.

"Maybe, and I say that based on a pattern. Historically, Black groups have always been infiltrated, and rated on by one of their own people."

"So you believe that it's just a matter of time?" asks Taylor. "If Blacks are involved yes."

At the shopping mall, Sakinah, Jada, and her first cousin Raquel are in a top of the line lingerie store looking at all sorts of sexy things to wear. "Jada, you think my baby will like this?" asks Sakinah, while holding up a gray satin gown.

"That's all right, but, girl, you need to get a collection of these in assorted flavors." Jada holds up a powder blue lace teddy.

"Roc, you like this?" she asks.

"Yeah, they're all right for old married couples, but if you really want to spice up your life, try wearing the stockings and garder belts."

"Sakinah, don't pay any attention to little Ms. Aphrodisiac. If you really want some spice wear these. Crotchless." Jada holds the panties up and they all burst out laughing.

It's early evening and Malik is in the courtroom of Judge C. W. Bey requesting a six month continuance. Aunt Pat is there and also the client, the CEO of Mahogany Cosmetic. "Your honor, my client, Mahogany, alleges copyright infringement against the defendant in regards to their line of facial scrub products. My client believes that the chemical formula utilized by the defendants in their product was stolen from my client and given to the defendants by person's inside Mahogany."

The defendant's attorney jumps to his feet. "Your Honor, this is utter nonsense. My client, Sun Beach, has no known association with anyone at Mahogany. Not only this, but Sun Beach employs their own team of chemist to create their product line."

"Your Honor, we requested documentation of Sun Beach's records showing development and research on these facial scrubs prior to the completion of the formula at Mahogany."

"And what were your findings?" the judge asks. "We never received any of those reports with the discovery material."

The judge beams over at the defense table.

"And why is that, Mr. Feagin?"

"Your Honor, that was done I believe to safe guard trade secrets."

"That doesn't make any sense. If both companies already have the formula for the exact same product, then there are no secrets is there? The question is the date of product development and completion. Right?"

"Yes, Your Honor."

"I'm ordering that production records be turned over to the plaintiff immediately, is that under stood Mr. Bernard Feagin!"

"Yes, Your Honor."

"Good, this court is adjourned!" Judge Bey slams his gavel down and exits the bench. Aunt Pat claps lightly before standing and kissing Malik on the cheek. "Great job, I'm buying you dinner!" she says. Malik smiles then notices his client, Jo Ann Amos.

"Just give me a moment, Auntie."

Malik walks over to his client, a very beautiful dark-skinned woman with high cheek bones, large dark eyes, and a picture-perfect white smile. She's stylish, no question about that, wearing a tan business suit with large gold buttons, and gold silk four-inch heels to match.

"Ms. Amos." She cut's him off. "I've asked you to call me Jo Ann, we can be on first-name bases, can't we?"

"Yes, we can."

"You were simply marvelous today! I almost had an orgasm watching you."

Malik smiles, not sure how to respond to that. "Thank you," he says.

"Uh, before I leave, I just wanted you to know that I believe we are going to win this thing, I believe they lied, that they did not turn over those papers because they have none."

"Is it possible for them to just make up some now since they have the formula?"

"Yes, that's possible but unlikely."

"Why do you think that? If they will steal, they certainly won't have a problem covering this up."

"Stealing is one thing, but finding a team of chemist to come in here before the Judge and lie on the stand is another matter altogether."

"I see the point."

"I will be in touch as soon as I hear anything from the court."

"Thank you, I'm so happy to have you on my side." Malik shakes Ms. Amos's hand then walks back over to the plaintiff's table where his auntie is waiting. He gathers up his files, placing them inside his briefcase before taking his aunt's hand and leading her out the courtroom.

Twenty minutes later, Aunt Pat and Malik are sitting at their favorite eatery having one of Malik's favorite meals. Stuffed jumbo shrimp with crab meat. "You have adjusted quite well," says Aunt Pat.

"I've always been a fast learner and I believe that I get my strength from you and mom."

"You're a chip off the old block for sure. How is Sakinah doing?"

"Sakinah is doing well. Sometimes I come home and find her asleep in the children's room, though."

"She was so good with those two."

"Yes, she was." Malik looks off into the distance for a moment at the memory. "So when are you going to make me a great-aunt again." Aunt Pat smiles and so does Malik.

"Soon, we are working on it, Sakinah wants more children."

"Oh yeah, I think that's great."

"Yeah, she called earlier and told me that she allowed Jada and Roc to talk her into buying a number of different outfits to wear at bed time. And some of them crotchless."

They both laugh. "I bet those were my daughter's idea."

"Most likely."

"Jada says that Sakinah kept most of the children's clothing, is that true?"

"She and Mom went through their things together. They want Kazi and Eunique's new brothers and sisters to know about them, what happened to them and why."

"That's understandable," says Aunt Pat.

It's 9:00 p.m., exactly three hours since Malik made it home from dinner with Aunt Pat, and FBI Agents Branch and Oliver are sitting in a car down the block from his home. "You think he's in for the night?" asks Oliver.

"Let's hope so."

"What do you mean by that?" Branch doesn't respond.

"Look, you have not made a secret of the fact that you are cheering for this guy."

"Cheering for who? What guy? What has he done? Tell me one piece of evidence that we have showing his involvement in this.

There is none! We are here outside his home based on a theory of retribution, some racist old hag claims she heard stated!"

"We have done more for less."

"That may be true, however never in a case where we had someone who was a clear victim."

"It's the children, isn't it?" Oliver asks.

"What about them?"

"It's why you are cheering for this guy."

"Understand one thing, I'm not cheering for anyone. However, I sat at the bar watching this man holding his dead kids in his arms with half their skulls blown off, soaked in blood. Now, I ask myself, was the death of those children necessary. My answer, NO! I then go to the scene of Klans men and Aryans lynched and blown apart. People who spread hate and violence. People responsible according to ballistics on the gun taken from Mr. Reckless, for the murder of those two children and countless others, and I ask myself honestly, is the death of these people necessary, and I have to say yes, it is. It reminds me of what Malcolm X said about 'The Chickens coming home to roost.' As I recall, he said it never made him sad either."

"But is this the way to do it?" Oliver asks.

"Granted it's against the law and raises a moral question. And that's why we are sitting here. But until someone comes up with a legal way to rid society of this growing cancer, it's the only one we have, and it seems to be working."

It's the next morning and Malik is sitting in his office when the phone rings. "Would you excuse me a moment, Mr. Webb."

"Sure, would you like for me to step out?"

"Oh no, that's not necessary. Bell, Harris and Davenport, Mr. Davenport speaking. Scoot, how are you? Is that right? No, no problems as of yet. Thought I'd seen some of the same people more than once. What about the phone? Okay, hey, Scoot, give my regards to Karen."

Hanging up, Malik turns back to his client. "Now, Mr. Webb, you were saying that your company would like to put this firm on retainer?"

"That's exactly what I said, my father used to work on your grandfathers house before he passed. He was a good man." Mr. Webb goes on talking as Malik sit's back in his chair distracted.

Across town, Captain Twyman is sitting in his office going over paper work when the phone rings, he picks it up. "Captain Twyman. When, where? Okay." The captain hangs up, then rushes out of his office looking for Lieutenant Jackson. He finds him going over the patrol logs. "Jackson, could you come into my office for a minute?"

"Sure, Captain."

Jackson walks inside and takes a seat. The captain closes the door before turning to Jackson. "There has been another murder over in Macon, Georgia, in broad daylight. Witnesses say that it was a sniper. A single shot to the head."

"What does that have to do with us?"

"The guy was David Shook, a Grand Dragon in the Klan."

The captain gives Jackson a moment to put it together. "Oh, shit! You think it's related to what we have going on here?"

"Could be. Assign a couple of our detectives to run over there and see what they can find out. I'll give the Sheriff over there a call and let him know they are coming and why!"

"Okay," says Jackson. He then stands to leave, but turns back to the captain. "Looks like this thing is going to get worse before it gets better." He then walks out the door closing it behind him, leaving Twyman to ponder over the scope of what's taking place.

Sakinah and Hugh Lamont are sitting in her driveway as she gathers up all the bags from her shopping spree. "Thanks for taking me to the store, I don't know what's wrong with my car, I'll have Malik look at it when he gets home." Hugh ignores what she just said. "I know that you are aware of what Malik is doing!" Sakinah stops and looks at him not sure that she has heard him correctly.

"What the hell did you say!"

"I said that you know what Malik is doing!"

"What are you talking about?"

"Come on, don't play stupid, you are not good at it!"

"So stop asking stupid questions!"

"What if these people start killing black men because of what's going on? Some Klansmen was killed over in Georgia today."

"Since when have they stopped?" Sakinah removes the rest of her bags from the back of the car then slams the door shut. Hugh sits there watching her going into the house before slowly backing out the driveway.

Malik is leaving the office, as he passes by the reception desk he stops to say good night to Janice. "Did you hear about someone shooting the Klan leader over in Georgia today?" she asks.

"No, I didn't."

"The reporter says that his death may be related to those killings here?"

"That's something to think about. Well, good night, Janice, be safe."

"You too, Mr. Davenport."

As Malik is leaving the building, Detectives Taylor and Brooks are sitting in a Burger King parking lot across the street. "Well, we know for sure that he wasn't in Georgia today," says Taylor. "Let's head to the station, I'm sure the chief is waiting to hear this."

Malik is pulling up in front of his home having left his office twenty minutes earlier. He blows the horn once, and Sakinah walks out closing the door behind her. She walks over to where Malik is waiting and gets into the car.

"Hi, beautiful," says Malik. He leans over and gives her a kiss on the lips.

"Umm, you smell so good!"

"Thanks."

"What's wrong? Live jazz and dinner are your favorites," says Malik.

"I know." Sakinah sits in silence watching the scenery go by.

"Hugh Lamont is an asshole!" she blunts out.

"Yes, he is," Malik agrees. "I don't trust him."

"Neither do I."

"Be careful around him baby," warns Sakinah.

"Always." They ride the rest of the way to the club in silence, holding hands, each lost in their own thoughts. Once arriving at the jazz club, Malik selects a table where they have a great view of the stage. As they await the band to the stage, they make small talk. "Did what happen in Georgia today have anything to do with you?"

"I told you that I was putting some distance between all of this and myself, but I never said it was over."

"I know, I'm just asking."

"Sweet Scoot called me at the office today and told me that the Feds were tailing me and that they slept outside our home the other night."

"What?"

"I don't know about you but I feel a whole lot safer." Malik takes her hand as they turn their attention to the MC taking the stage. "Hello, everyone and welcome to open mic Night at the legendary Jazz Club lavern williams. I am your MC for the evening, your hostess with the Mostess. Perry Pondexter!"

The standing room only crowd gives him an extended round of applause. "Thank you! Thank you!" he says.

"I like him, he dresses so smartly," says Sakinah. "You can't go wrong with a tailored, black, single-breasted after six," says Malik.

"Now coming to the stage, a very special gift from Houston, Texas, one of the jewels in a renowned musical family. Please give her a warm Alabama welcome, Ms. Eloise Laws!"

"Miss Eloise Laws! Show her, love ya'll," yells Perry.

Eloise walks onto the stage smiling and bowing to the crowd, who have all stood up. "Thank you so much. Thank you, thank you so much!" she says.

"Isn't that the criminal profiler?" Sakinah asks, turning to Malik as the audience continued with its applause.

"Yes, that's her—wow! I know the name, the family. Her brother Hubert is one of the original jazz crusaders and her brother Ronnie Laws is one of the best sax players in the business. Wow!" Malik says, stunned. "I want to meet her. I want to thank her for helping us," whispers Sanikah into Malik's ear.

"Okay, after the show," says Malik before turning his full attention to the stage.

"Hello, Mobile, and thank you for such a warm welcome. I'd like to sing one of my favorite songs for you. It's called 'When I Fall in Love.' It's dedicated to a very special friend of mine. We met like two ships passing in the night...many years passed before I would see him again."

The audience claps for her briefly then dies down. Eloise takes a seat on the stool, pulls the mic up close to her as her band begins to play. Sakinah takes Malik's hand into hers then lays her head on his shoulder as Eloise sings. "When I fall in love it will be forever, or I'll never fall in love."

JoAnn Amos is sitting in the office with Malik, early afternoon the next day. Malik is still feeling the effects of staying out with Sakinah last night listening to the new local jazz talent to 1:00 a.m. "As I was telling you over the phone JoAnn, Sun Beach is unable to produce the documents and reports we requested, so they want to settle."

"Does that mean that they will acknowledge that they stole the formula?"

"Well, not exactly, and that's where the problem comes in. You see in order for you to safeguard future projects, it's important to your company to identify the insider. But if Sun Beach does so, they indirectly imply that they obtained the formula from the source."

"So what do we do?"

"I think we should settle the matter out of court. That would mean dropping the suit."

"I don't see that as an advantage."

"Well, actually it is. You see, by settling out of court we can draw up an agreement prior to the settlement, where they will agree to give us the insider, remove the product from the shelves and pay your company a handsome sum without having to place all of this on the record in court."

"Do you trust them?"

"I will keep a copy of the agreement here at the firm and if they do not live up to what's contained in it we are back in court on both issues."

"What amount are they willing to settle for?"

"Fifty million."

"What about eighty?"

"Eighty it is. I'll get back with Mr. Feagin sometime today and see if we can get the paperwork drawn up. I'll need to reach you quickly for a signing."

"Here is my pager number, if I'm not at the office."

"Okay, well that's it for now, thanks for your business," says Malik. He and Jo'Ann shake hands. "My pleasure."

"Let me see you out." Malik leads her out of his office and down to the lobby next to where Janice is working. Jo'Ann continues to the doors, leading out the building. "Janice, get Attorney Bernard Feagin on the phone for me please."

"Okay, just a moment," she says, before searching through her rolerdex for the number. "Let me know when you reach him." Malik turns and walks back to his office, closing the door, before going and stretching out on the black leather love seat. He rests there momentarily before jumping up suddenly and dialing a number on his phone.

"As Salamu Alaikum Hasheem. How are you my brother? Real busy, but I like it. Listen, tell Amin everything is Lima-Charlie, so says the sweet one. Tell him that the big hat boys have joined the game. Islam."

Malik hangs up the phone then falls back in his chair. A moment later, his phone rings, he picks it up. "Yes, Janice?"

"Mr. Feagin is on line three."

"Thanks, Janice." Malik clears his throat before switching to line three and picking up. "Mr. Feagin, today is your lucky day, but it's going to cost you eighty million!" he says.

It's early evening and Agents Branch and Oliver are walking into Chief Jacocks's office with really nothing to report on the murders or their connection to Malik. "Just the two agents I was looking for. Have a seat and read this," says the chief, handing both gray folders.

"Whats this?" Branch asks.

"It's the report on the murdered Klansmen over in Georgia. Last week!"

The chief moves around to the front of his desk and takes a seat. "One shot to the left frontal lobe?" says Branch.

"Exactly! No witnesses, no sound, no suspicious persons in the area," says Jacocks.

"I'm beginning to believe that we have a group of mercenaries behind this," says Oliver. "Check this out."

Chief hands them another gray folder. "I did a background check on Mr. Davenport, including his military experience. "What did you come up with?" asks Branch.

"Most of it is in the file. Born leader, uncommon valor, fearless in Na'am, intelligent, a sniper, in fact he was the highest shooter in the Second Marine division H&S Company while there. I spoke with a couple of ex-commanding officers and they told me that Mr. Davenport was fiercely loved by his comrades, and that any problem with him, was a problem with them."

"Do you think that he is still in touch with some of those men?" asks Oliver.

"The officers I spoke to said that they would bet their lives on it. And they said that all his real friends are deadly."

"So maybe there is no need for him to go to Georgia or any-where else huh?" Oliver suggests.

"That's very possible, it's also why I'm compiling this file on Mr. Davenports friends. This is Amin Shakur, AKA Marvin Grant a Chicago native. We have no known address on him at the present. He's the back to nature type. Strong, intelligent and very loyal to Mr. Davenport. For sure these two are in contact. This is Pup AKA Andrew Manigault. He's pro-black, intelligent, expert close combat fighter and he's also very close to Mr. Davenport. He's a Baltimore native, Mr. Davenport's homey. This is Joseph Thomas AKA Monk. He and Mr. Davenport were roommates at camp LeJune. The two of them are very close, in fact, I was told that when Mr. Davenport left the core, he gave Mr. Thomas his lucky sling that he used on his M16. I'm told he still has it. He is from Patterson New Jersey. This is Kethon Jones, AKA Terrible-T. A cold blooded killer. He's also an expert with explosives and small automatic weapons."

"Explosives were used in that murder of the people in the barn," says Oliver. "His specialty. He's from Detroit," says the chief. This is Gary McGuirrie, AKA Pasqually. He's special forces trained, expert with weapons, close combat fighting and he's very loyal to Mr. Davenport also, he's from Atlanta, Georgia. This is Edwin Harris, AKA Cuddy, he's from Galena, Maryland, and he has the same qualifications as the others, and a very quick temper. Last but not least this is Johnny Sanders, AKA Ant-Head. He's from Chicago. He's a sniper."

"Mr. Davenport has a very impressive array of friends." Oliver is clearly excited over the background information. "But do you have anything linking them to these crimes. Because I have a few ex-Marine core buddies that I'm still in touch with who have special forces training, close combat, automatic weapons and explosive training. But that does not mean that they go around killing people. Oh, and two of them are snipers," says Branch.

Chief Jacocks moves back around his desk and takes a seat. "Would you like to be reassigned?" he asks.

"No, I would not."

"Good! Then I suggest you keep an open mind to this investigation and handle it in a professional manner."

"Yes, sir."

"Now I want you two to busy yourself on trying to get a location on all these men, is that a problem?"

"No, it's not, we'll get right on top of it. Oh, and if they are located what then?" asks Oliver. "Give them room and set up surveillance."

"Ten-four," says Oliver, he and Branch stand and walk out the Chiefs office, taking the gray folders with them.

Ms. Norma is home sitting in her living room speaking with her girlfriend Martha Mosley while watching a game show. "Did you see all my children today?" Martha asks.

"No, girl. I was down at the market talking to Rose Feagin and Elizabeth Curry and missed my bus."

"I was hoping you could tell me what happened. I laid back in the chair to rest my eyes for a minute and girl when I looked up, it was six o'clock, I had dozed off." They both laugh.

"I've been doing that alot myself lately. You know I refused to take all that diabetic medication and I feel so much better. But some days I get really tired," says Ms. Norma.

"You've got to make sure you get plenty iron then. Eat a lot of spinach," Martha suggests.

"I do, that's why I go to the market every day and get my vegetables fresh."

"That's the best way, I don't like all those can foods either," says Martha.

As they are watching the television a special news report flashes across the screen, interrupting the regular scheduled programming, Martha sees it and asks Ms. Norma to turn up the volume which she does. They both listen carefully.

"Oh, girl, they done killed another one of those White Power guys in North Carolina today. What is the world coming to?" Martha asks.

"We'll just have to wait and see, that's all we can do," says Ms. Norma.

Captains Twyman and Sissy, his sketch artist, are working late tonight because of all the interviews and statements taken from crime scene witnesses. She knocks on the captain's door then rushes inside. "Captain, there has been another killing of a white supremacist in Jacksonville, North Carolina. Same circumstances."

"Damn! Get Lieutenant Jackson in here!"

"Right away!" Sissy rushes back out the door calling for the lieutenant.

On the other side of town, Malik has decided to have an evening swim with Kevin as Sakinah and Lenora sit watching them splashing and diving in the water. "Kevin thinks of Malik as his dad," says Lenora.

"They really enjoy each other. Did you know Malik told Kevin he's buying him a car when he gets his license?"

"Yes, that's all Kevin's been talking about. He can't wait to grow up now," says Lenora, she and Sakinah smile at Kevin's innocence. The phone rings and Sakinah goes and answers it.

"Hello. Yes, he is, who's calling? Oh, hold on."

Sakinah walks back out by the pool. "Malik, telephone."

"Who is it?"

"They say a friend?" Malik gets out the pool, after picking Kevin up and tossing him.

"Yea!" screams Kevin. Malik then makes his way into the house. "Hello. What can I do for you? Sure, I'll be there in thirty minutes." Malik hangs up the phone then sticks his head outside the door. "I've got to make a run. Kev, I'll have to finish you off later."

"See you later," says Kevin before diving under the water. Malik runs upstairs and changes into dry clothes, then rushes out the door. Within thirty minutes, he's sitting in a booth at a small out of the way diner by the Fredrick Douglas off ramp when Agent Branch walks in and takes a seat. The two men sit and look at each other a moment. "How are you, Agent Branch?"

"I'm okay, can we find a seat in the back somewhere?"

"Sure," says Malik.

Both men stand, and Agent Branch spots a table in a far corner more to his liking and they sit there. Agent Branch slides a black folder over to Malik. "Do you know any of these men?" he asks.

Malik looks at the photos of Amin and the others. "Why?" he asks.

"Listen up because we don't have a lot of time. The agency is looking for these men, people in it believe that they and you may be behind these killings. Am I making myself clear?"

"I."

Agent Branch puts up his hand silencing Malik before he can answer. "I've wrestled with my conscience over this ever since these murders began, and though I know it's against the law, I know that something has to be done about these hateful people. What,

I don't know, so until I figure that out you've got a pass from me. Understand?"

"I think I do."

"Semper Fi," says Agent Branch and with that he stands and walks out. Malik sits there, puzzled, not knowing what to think regarding what just took place. He reaches inside his wallet, removes ten dollars and places it under the salt shaker for the hard working waitress just for taking up the table space before he too walks out.

It's the next morning and Malik is sitting in his office when Jada rushes in unannounced followed by her mother. "Knock! Knock!" says Jada with a smile.

"Uh, looks like you're already inside," says Malik, grinning at his outlandish cousin.

"Mom and I want to know if you and Sakinah are going to the family REUNION?"

"We are planning on it."

"Good," says Jada before sitting down on the corner of the desk. "Then Mom and I are riding with you, guys."

"She says I drive too slow. I told her that you and Sakinah may want to enjoy the drive together," says Auntie Pat.

"Mom, they been together since junior high school, they need a break," says Jada as she moves around to the back of Malik and gives him a hug. "Okay, let's get out of here so that Malik can get back to work."

"Malik, did you hear about the White Klan leader being killed in North Carolina?" Jada asks.

"Yes, I heard."

"At least that business has moved on from here. Come on, girl!" says Aunt Pat before pulling Jada by the arm toward the door. "You know I love you don't you cuz!" says Jada.

"I know, I love you too."

"Remember that!" says Jada before allowing her mom to take her out the office and down the hall. Malik picks up his phone then dials a number, then waits. "Hasheem. Islam Mo, listen get a message to the brothers. Tell them that the big hat boys got photos and are looking for the entire platoon. We've got one on our side who says the light is green, but it may not last. Tell Lil-C to complete his mission. From then on we're in a holding pattern. Shukran."

"(Thanks)" says Malik before hanging up.

It's lunchtime and Malik is having it with an old college buddy named Hector Delgado. A Puerto Rican playboy from New York, turned political activist after almost being killed by the husband of a Egyptian beauty that he was sleeping around with. The husband, a very wealthy and powerful man, knew too many people in the city of New York to remain Hector's playground, so he moved to the South.

"I'm telling you Malik," says Hector, "you should think about it, because you have what it takes, the look, the personality, the money, the family structure. Everything is in place for you."

"Ah, I don't know Hector, I've never really gave a lot of thought to running for any type of office. Politics is not one of my specialties."

"That's bullshit and we both know it. Everything is political, we just call those things by other names, and believe me I know."

Malik says nothing; he's watching a beautiful woman walking up to their table smiling a gorgeous smile, with big doe eyes. Hector sees her and stands up smiling himself.

"Carmen!" says Hector. The two of them tightly embrace, then kiss each other lightly on the lips. "Malik Davenport, this is Carmen Davis, ex-circuit court Judge, now running for Mayor of Mobile."

"It's a pleasure to meet you Your Honor," says Malik. The two shake hands. "Hector, you told me that he was charming and handsome, I'm pleased to find that true. But please, call me Carmen. I've been off the bench, a couple of years now."

The three of them take their seats, Malik pulls out the chair for Carmen. "Oh, thank you," she says.

"Was there any particular reason that you left the court?" Malik asks.

"Basically, it was to restricting, if I'm going to grow old, I'd rather do it out in the open, moving around, enjoying life, versus being locked behind chamber doors and a stack of appeal briefs." The three of them laugh.

"I see your point," says Malik.

"She doesn't look a day over twenty-nine," Hector says jokingly.

"Would you stop?" Carmen taps Hector on the back of his hand. "You can't blame a brother for trying. Anyway back to the matter at hand, Mr. Davenport here says that he's not cut out for politics."

Carmen turns to Malik. "Is that true?"

"It's just something I've never gave a lot of thought to."

"Well, I think you should. Polls show that I stand a good chance of winning this election and I'd like to bring someone in with your corporate knowledge, because running this city is a business. From what Hector has told me, you are very active in the community, and you've already established three or four charities?"

"That's true, however I done that solely with the intent of providing opportunities for those less fortunate than myself. I believe with the proper molding, most of the destructive unrest among our youth can be reversed into positive building."

"My feelings exactly," says Carmen.

"Hector, I like him."

Carmen sits back in her chair, admiring Malik, and thinking where in city government he'd be best suited. "I told you that he's the man for the job, even though he doesn't know it yet." They all laugh. "I just want to hear you say that you will think about it?" says Carmen.

"I will," says Malik.

Sakinah has just returned home from a doctor's appointment and is on the phone with Ms. Norma. "Mom, I'm out of breath, I just walked through the door and guess what? She told me that I'm PREGNANT! Yes, I was so excited, I cried all the way home. No, I haven't told Malik, he, Jada and I are having lunch together tomorrow INSHALLAH, and I plan to tell him then. Okay I will. Thanks, Mom. I love you too."

As Sakinah is hanging up the phone, Malik is walking in the door. He goes over to her and gives her a kiss. "Hello, sexy," he says, then pulls back to look at her.

"What's wrong?" he asks.

"Nothing, I'm just happy." Sakinah gives Malik a big smile and another kiss. "So happy that you are crying? Who was that on the phone?"

"Your mom."

"Oh, that explains it."

"Not really, but God-willing, I will tell you all about it tomorrow. We are having lunch with Jada."

"Don't remind me!" says Malik with a smile. He then sits down on the end of the sofa and pulls Sakinah down onto his lap and kisses her again. But Sakinah really lays a kiss on him. "Wow! Are you horny?" Malik asks, giving her the once-over.

"No, I mean yes, but mostly just happy. And what I'm going to tell you tomorrow is going to make you very happy also."

Sakinah kisses him lightly on his forehead.

"Oh yea? Well tell me now."

"Nope!"

"Guess who I had lunch with today?"

"It had better not been another woman!"

"It was, a very beautiful older woman at that. You know rumor has it that they are better lovers."

"Don't make me clown on you."

Sakinah gives Malik her best stern look and he laughs. "I'm just kidding, but I did have lunch with a beautiful lady and my old friend Hector Delgado."

"How is Hector?"

"Still scheming. Anyway, he set up this lunch date between retired Judge Carmen Davis and me."

"Isn't she running for mayor?"

"Yes she is, and she wants me on her team."

"That's wonderful!" says Sakinah, as she beams with pride. "What did you say?"

"I told her that I would think about it."

"I think you should, I've always wanted to be the wife of a US Senator, and this could be the beginning of that trip. I can dress up and plan big parties for US Congress members. Visit the White House. Oh, and by the way I don't like that name 'White House.'

The person who thought of that must have been a dummy, it was white, so he named it that! Or was there a deeper meaning. Hum? Anyway, I can go shopping in Georgetown, I hear they have some really nice stores, and charge everything to your US Senate Bank Account."

Malik just sits there looking at his wife smiling, not wanting to interrupt her when she's on a roll. "Hold on a minute, I said I'd think about it. I didn't say anything about running for office."

"Whatever! You know what?"

"What?"

"I'm going upstairs and run you a nice warm bath, with candle-light. And while you are enjoying that and some Miles Davis live at the PlayBoy Jazz Festival, I'm going to come down here and fix your favorite meal, stuffed shrimp with crab meat inside, rice pilaf, broccoli with cheese sauce, with a slice of cheesecake I picked up from the bakery today!"

"You're too much!" Malik kisses the back of her hand. "I know, you don't deserve me." They smile together. "I'll call you when the bath is ready." An hour and a half later, Sakinah and Malik are again dinning together. She's wearing one of the silk teddy's she purchased while shopping with Jada and Roc. Malik has on only a pair of linen pajama bottoms.

"This is delicious!" says Malik.

"Like me?"

"Like you, baby." Malik slides his hand over Sakinah's thigh.

"I heard you and Jada whispering over the phone. What was that all about?"

"Just girl talk, some of which you will hear later."

"So what are you going to do, to keep my mind preoccupied until then?" Sakinah grins, gets up and walks over to Malik's chair, and turns him around. She then straddles him. "Oh, I can think of two or three things right off to occupy your mind with. But you can help me out if anything pops up, or comes to mind."

They kiss, Malik removes the straps of her top from both shoulders, and they kiss even harder.

"Bad girl," says Malik. He then lifts Sakinah up and sits her down on the countertop.

It's eleven thirty the next morning and Jada, Sakinah, and Malik are walking out the door of his home when the phone rings. Malik goes back inside to answer it, it's Hugh Lamont.

"Hello, what! I'm on my way to lunch with two lovely ladies. Can't this wait? This had better be important!" Malik slams the phone down.

"That was your brother. He says that he needs to talk with me that it's urgent."

"Where is he? Why didn't he just come over?"

"Cause he's a punk!" says Jada. "He's at that spot on the hill in the park, where we used to hang out at."

"Why does he want you to come out there?"

"Maybe the fresh air and tree's help to clear his mind. Anyways, listen, you two go ahead in Jada's car and I'll meet you there." Sakinah walks over and kisses him.

"Don't be long," she says.

"I won't."

"Tell Hugh Lamont, that I said that he's a punk!" Jada and Sakinah get in her car and pull off. Malik gets into his and drives off in the opposite direction. Fifteen minutes later, he is parking his car, getting out, and walking up the path and into the clearing where he finds Hugh waiting.

"What's so important that you had to drag me all the way out here?" Malik is furious.

"It's over, Malik," says Hugh Lamont softly. "What's over, what the hell are you talking about!"

"The killing!"

Suddenly from all around Malik, white men come out from the bushes carrying guns and clubs, and circle him.

Malik instinctively spreads his feet and bends his knees getting into a fighting stance.

"So this is the Nigger been doing all the killing?" says the leader of the group.

"Don't call me a Nigger, my name is MALIK DAVENPORT."

"Ooh, he's one of those upperty niggers too." The Klan leader looks at Hugh Lamont.

"Gone get out of here boy, we'll take it from here." Hugh Lamont and Malik lock eyes momentarily as an opening is made in the circle and Hugh Lamont walks through it. "Well, Nigger, it's just you and all of us now."

Malik closes his eyes, seeing his wife, and children. At that moment, Sakinah is sitting outside the café downtown Mobile, laughing and smiling with Jada. "I hope it's a girl," says Jada excitedly.

"Girl, I'm giving my baby another son." Sakinah picks up her glass of orange juice to drink from it when she feels an overwhelming sense that Malik is in danger. She drops the glass stands up and screams. "Malik!" The glass shatters as she grabs Jada's keys them runs to her car.

Back in the woods Malik opens his eyes. "Fuck you, you rotten teeth bitch!"

A Klansmen walks up from behind Malik and hits him in the rib cage with a bat, Malik falls to the ground.

"No, fuck you, nigger!"

Sakinah is driving wildly, speeding, weaving in and out of traffic, blowing the horn and crying. "I'm coming, baby, I'm coming. Just hold on!" She pulls over to the curb where a pay phone sits empty and runs to it dropping coins into it and waits. "Amin! Malik is in trouble. He's at the hill with Hugh Lamont. I just know!" Jada is on the pay phone crying, talking to her mother.

"I don't know Mom, just call the police or somebody. I'm getting a cab?"

Jada hangs up the phone then runs into the street. Back on the hill Malik is doubled over on the ground bleeding from his face and head. His shirt is torn half off and covered in blood. He moves to stand up, yells, then runs and tackles two of the Klansmen, throwing blows to both of their bodies and faces. Their friends rush over and begin kicking and clubbing Malik off the two.

"Damn! That Nigger is strong!" says one of the two whom Malik was pounding.

"Bring me that rope!" he yells.

Sissy Bonner rushes into the captain's office. "Captain, we just received a call from Mr. Davenport's aunt, Pat, she says that he needs police assistance out at the Hill."

"Well, get some people out there. Call Taylor and Brooks and have my driver bring my car out front!" the captain orders.

Amin, Nino, Pup, Terrible, Pasqually, Monk, Cuddy, and Ant-Head have loaded the last of their weapons in the van and are closing the van door. "Let's go!" yells Amin. "If someone has hurt my brother, a whole lot of people are going to die!" he says. Everyone sit's back quietly checking their weapons. Agents Branch and Oliver have just gotten the call. "Where is that located?" Branch asks.

"I've got it," he says.

"How far?" asks Oliver. "About three miles." Oliver turns on his red flashing lights, and speed toward the park.

Back at the Hill, the Klansmen have the rope around Malik's neck and are dragging him. Malik is struggling against the rope and blocking blows, as they continue to beat him. "Come on, Nigger Boy, it's time to go see your ancestors."

Ms. Norma is in the car with Aunt Pat. "Lord God, please don't let nothing happen to my baby!" Aunt Pat takes her hands.

"He's fine, ain't nothing going to happen to him, all this may be for nothing," Jada says that they were just sitting there and Sakinah jumped up and ran out!

"She's pregnant, she can feel when something is wrong with her baby's father. She can feel it!" says Ms. Norma.

Back on the Hill, the Klansmen have finally dragged Malik over to an old oak tree. "Tie his hands behind his back!" he yells. Malik is struggling against having his hands tied behind his back when one of the Klansmen with work boots on steps back, then kicks Malik full force into his testicles. Malik falls over face down. "You punk ass motherfuckers, it's not over, you're going to die, all of you for this, you're going to die!"

Malik begins choking on his own blood, he coughs, trying to clear his throat. He's growing weaker.

"Shut the fuck up, ain't no one else dying around here but you shit for brains. Strip the rest of those clothes. This nigga got balls. I think I'll take 'em as a trophy."

Sakinah has arrived in the parking lot, she sees Malik's JAG, and pulls up next to it. She blows the horn, then gets out running toward the path! "I'm here baby! I'm here, hold on!" says Sakinah. On the Hill, Malik hears the horn and smiles in spite of himself.

"Throw the rope over the tree. Someone is coming, hurry up!" says the Klansmen.

Sakinah is now on the path, running as fast as she can, pushing tree branches out the way. "Malik! Malik!" she screams as she nears the clearing.

Amin and the boys have just arrived, they jump out the van and run toward the path leading to the Hill. "It's game time, motherfuckers!" yells Cuddy.

Jada is in the cab. "Can you please drive a little faster?"

"I'm doing sixty now."

"Well, go faster, I'll pay the ticket."

"It's your money."

Ms. Norma, Aunt Pat, Captain Twyman, Detectives Taylor and Brooks, several police units and Agents Oliver and Branch all pull up in the parking lot, one after the other. "Something has happened to my baby," says Ms. Norma.

"Spread out!" yells the captain to his officers. They pull their weapons before running off in all directions looking for Malik.

Sakinah has reached the end of the path opening to the clearing. She sees Malik, naked, beaten, and bloody, hung by his neck. "No, baby, NO! NO! NO! You can't leave me." Sakinah falls to her knees. "You have a son, Malik, I was going to tell you at the café."

Behind her, Amin and the boys rush into the clearing, heavily armed. Then Agents Branch and Oliver, the captain behind them, and finally Ms. Norma and Aunt Pat. They all stand there in horror, unable to believe what they are witnessing. Not only was Malik brutally beaten, but someone cut his penis off and placed it into his mouth. Aunt Pat is holding Ms. Norma, keeping her on her feet. "Look what they've done to my baby. Look what they done to my beautiful baby!"

"Damn!" says Terrible-T.

"DOUBLE-CROSSED!"

DON'T MISS DOUBLE CROSS II.

COMING SOON.

HERE IS A PREVIEW:

It's late evening, Sweet Scoot and Karen are sitting in a swank supper club.

"Have you seen the baby yet?" she asks.

"No, not yet. I plan to drop by later this week, though. I know Sakinah is exhausted after all this. She put up a strong front because that's what Malik was about, strength. But I know she's hurting and tired. She needs some time to herself.

"You think she'd mind if I volunteered to watch MJ while she relaxes?"

"I'm sure that she wouldn't, but I don't think she wants to let that little guy out of her sight for a while. And if she did, I think you'd have to get in line. There are a lot of people that want a piece of that little guy."

"Yes, I see your point, but be sure to let her know that I'm here if she needs me."

"I will. Sakinah will be happy just knowing that you feel that way."

"I really liked Malik. He took on a lot of other people's problems who will never even know."

"Including the police," says Sweet Scoot with a grin.

"Oh yeah?" Karen studies him.

"Yes, they don't know that Malik was involved in the murders. They know that he was lured there by Hugh Lamont, but they don't know why."

"What happened to him, Hugh Lamont, that fucker!" Karen is upset at just the mention of his name.

"The police believe that Malik's killers may have kidnapped him, probably killed him, then dumped his body." Sweet Scoot leans back in his chair and smiles.

"But that's not what you believe, is it?" As Karen gives Scooter a penetrating stare, his pager goes off. He checks the number. "I'll be right back."

Scoot walks over to where the phones are located then dials the number that's in the pager.

"Hello, Mark, how are you? Great, no, just having dinner with a friend. Have you found what we were looking for? East Baltimore, Chase St. Thank you." Scoot hangs up the phone then returns to where Karen is waiting and retakes his seat. "No, I believe he's in Baltimore, on Chase Street."

"Dang you are everywhere!" Scooter pauses for a moment then jumps up and walks back over to the pay phone where he drops a couple of coins in then dials a number and waits.

"Amin, I'm good, just spoke to Mark, old boy is in East Baltimore, Chase Street, 1310. Right on!"

Again, Scoot hangs up the phone and returns to where Karen is waiting and takes his seat. He picks up his glass in a toast; Karen joins him. "Goodbye, Hugh Lamont!"

"And good riddance!" says Karen before she and Sweet Scoot sip their champagne.

ABOUT THE AUTHOR

Pasha was born in Mobile, Alabama. He is a United States Marine veteran and a college graduate with a degree in business computer systems. Pasha believes that the entire earth is his home and all mankind are family. His ability to write, he says, is a direct gift from God.

CPSIA information can be obtained
at www.ICGtesting.com
Printed in the USA
BVHW071923100621
609270BV00003B/286